## "YOU CAN TAKE ME OUT TO DINNER LATER. I NEVER SAID I WAS SLEEPY, DEAR."

Longarm reached up to turn off the gas jet by the door, but not before he'd noticed she was built like an hourglass indeed, as she sat on the bed in her black lace unmentionables. His move should have plunged the room into darkness, but it was almost bright as day outside. Her soft curves looked even better in the gloaming glow of gas street illumination. He didn't know what to say. So he just took off his own duds and climbed aboard.

"You told me New Yorkers like to get right to the point, Billie..."

*Also in the LONGARM series*
*from Jove*

LONGARM
LONGARM ON THE BORDER
LONGARM AND THE AVENGING
   ANGELS
LONGARM AND THE WENDIGO
LONGARM IN THE INDIAN NATION
LONGARM AND THE LOGGERS
LONGARM AND THE HIGHGRADERS
LONGARM AND THE NESTERS
LONGARM AND THE HATCHET MEN
LONGARM AND THE MOLLY
   MAGUIRES
LONGARM AND THE TEXAS
   RANGERS
LONGARM IN LINCOLN COUNTY
LONGARM IN THE SAND HILLS
LONGARM IN LEADVILLE
LONGARM ON THE DEVIL'S TRAIL
LONGARM AND THE MOUNTIES
LONGARM AND THE BANDIT QUEEN
LONGARM ON THE YELLOWSTONE
LONGARM IN THE FOUR CORNERS
LONGARM AT ROBBER'S ROOST
LONGARM AND THE SHEEPHERDERS
LONGARM AND THE GHOST
   DANCERS
LONGARM AND THE TOWN TAMER
LONGARM AND THE RAILROADERS
LONGARM ON THE OLD MISSION
   TRAIL

LONGARM AND THE DRAGON
   HUNTERS
LONGARM AND THE RURALES
LONGARM ON THE HUMBOLDT
LONGARM ON THE BIG MUDDY
LONGARM SOUTH OF THE GILA
LONGARM IN NORTHFIELD
LONGARM AND THE GOLDEN LADY
LONGARM AND THE LAREDO LOOP
LONGARM AND THE BOOT HILLERS
LONGARM AND THE BLUE NORTHER
LONGARM ON THE SANTA FE
LONGARM AND THE STALKING
   CORPSE
LONGARM AND THE COMANCHEROS
LONGARM AND THE DEVIL'S
   RAILROAD
LONGARM IN SILVER CITY
LONGARM ON THE BARBARY COAST
LONGARM AND THE MOONSHINERS
LONGARM IN PRISON
LONGARM IN BOULDER CANYON
LONGARM IN DEADWOOD
LONGARM AND THE LONE STAR
   LEGEND
LONGARM AND THE GREAT TRAIN
   ROBBERY
LONGARM IN THE BADLANDS
LONGARM IN THE BIG THICKET

TABOR EVANS

LONGARM

AND THE
EASTERN DUDES

A JOVE BOOK

LONGARM AND THE EASTERN DUDES

A Jove Book / published by arrangement with
the author

PRINTING HISTORY
Jove edition / November 1982

ISBN: 0-515-06250-2

Jove books are published by Jove Publications, Inc.,
200 Madison Avenue, New York, N. Y. 10016. The words
"A JOVE BOOK" and the "J" with sunburst are trademarks
belonging to Jove Publications, Inc.

PRINTED IN THE UNITED STATES OF AMERICA

# LONGARM

## AND THE EASTERN DUDES

# Chapter 1

By three o'clock in the morning there was a nip to the air of Denver, even in summer, and somewhere in the darkness the mysterious leaf burner Longarm had never caught was at it again. Folks who lived in Denver all the time said they didn't notice how their fair city seemed to be haunted all twelve months of the year by the faint scent of some fool roasting chestnuts or burning autumn leaves. But Longarm had just come down out of the Front Range, where the summer nights smelled of wild onion and pine, and as Denver's pungent perfume wafted up and down the alley it made him want to light the cold cheroot he was gripping with his teeth. But he didn't. A lawman staked out in an alley wasn't supposed to strike a match, take a leak, or do anything else that might give his position away.

One of the other lawmen hunkered behind the piled-up barricade of ash cans and trash barrels with Longarm started muttering about their superiors. "I tell you, boys, we've been sent on a fool's errand, and the sons of bitches who sent us are home snugabed for the night whilst we freeze our fool butts here."

Another growled, "That's for damn sure. It's going on three and I figured this for a bad tip in the first place."

Longarm didn't say anything. The men complaining were Treasury agents, so he didn't know them all that well. And besides, he suspicioned they could be right. He hadn't been there when that street informant tipped the Denver police that the Careful Corrigans meant to help themselves to the contents of the Denver Mint. But it did seem to Longarm that the city, state, and Federal authorities were a mite more excited than he'd have been about such a slim lead. The Careful Corrigans, as their nickname might indicate, had never in the past raided such an important target. And even if they had gone crazy with greed, Longarm knew there was only a fifty-fifty chance he and the others were staked out in the right alley.

The tip had been that the Careful Corrigans meant to blow the vaults of the Denver Mint building, period. The trouble was that there were two buildings in Denver that fit the description. There was the main mint over by Court Place and this infernal substation down on Market Street. Longarm's boss, Chief Marshal Billy Vail, was covering the main mint with the big shots from Treasury and the Colorado State Guard. Longarm and the smaller posse hunkered around him in the alley behind the substation had been an afterthought. The tip had come in after everyone had gone home for the day, so it had taken a spell to find out that, sure enough, they had a vault full of freshly coined money in this cellar, too.

One of the agents said, "Hell, the moon ball's riz and I can see the back door of the mint building clear as anything, now. How long are we supposed to wait about for nothing to happen?"

"Till something happens," a senior Treasury agent growled, "and stuff a sock in it. I know this is all kind of

2

new to you, but the idea of a stakeout is to surprise the other side with one's unexpected attendance at the scene of the crime. That ain't going to be easy if you keep making speeches."

Longarm nodded in silent approval as he shifted his weight and studied the massive back door across the alley in the moonlight. He was glad none of the deputies with him from Justice had needed chiding. Billy Vail had told Longarm he was in charge of the contingent from the U.S. Marshal's office. But Longarm didn't like to give orders any more than he liked taking them. So he'd told the boys with him just to do as the top kick from Treasury said, here. It was Treasury's vaults the Careful Corrigans were fixing to blow. Treasury had asked Justice for help, so it was Treasury's show.

A million years went by and all that happened was the moon got higher and the vision improved. Not a critter was stirring, not even the rats you sometimes noticed at night this close to the stockyards. The metal doors across the alley looked mighty solid and he could see now that they were solid bronze with a heroic steel bar padlocked across them.

Longarm heard someone whisper his name and muttered, "Over here." He turned to see Henry, the clerk who played the typewriter at the office, walking his way, tall. "Get your fool head down, Henry!" he growled. Henry gulped and ran the last few paces to crouch at Longarm's side in the shadows. Longarm saw that Henry was packing a Spencer Repeater. He wouldn't have been more surprised if the fussy clerk had been carrying a sewing machine, but he didn't comment.

Henry said, "Marshal Vail sent me to find out if anything's going on down this way."

Longarm shrugged and pointed with his chin at the solid-looking doorway across from them as he answered. "You'd have heard it twelve blocks off if anyone had made a serious attempt to get through that door, Henry."

"The team covering the front of the building hasn't seen or heard anything, either," Henry said. "Marshal Vail asked

3

me to ask you if you had any educated guesses to offer."

Longarm shrugged again. "This is a hell of a time to ask my opinion. I had second thoughts about the whole deal shortly after you dragged me away from the bar in the Black Cat this evening. The Careful Corrigans have hitherto confined their modest skills with dynamite to less imposing edifices."

Henry said, "Marshal Vail's worried about that, too. He says he knows the capabilities of the Careful Corrigans and that the brand of vaults Uncle Sam locks his money up in are awesome to contemplate blowing. He told me to tell you he just found out from Treasury that most of the coinage we're guarding is silver. He said you'd know what he meant."

Longarm nodded thoughtfully. "I'd already thought of that. The Frisco mint coins mostly gold pieces, which are what you might call a compact form of wealth, while the Denver mint here makes silver dollars, which ain't. Even if they managed to bust open the vaults here or up at the main mint, they'd need a team and wagon to tote off enough money to make it worth their while. As you can hear, if you listen, there ain't no wagons moving about over the cobbles at this hour."

The senior officer from Treasury had been listening, of course. He came over and joined them. "I follow your drift, Longarm. But what else can we do, save what we're doing?" he asked.

Longarm shrugged. "Nothing. The sun will come up in a few hours and we can all go home. You can go home, that is. Tomorrow morn shines on payday and I'm looking forward to a solvent weekend. They'd have never caught me on my own time for this fool chore had not I been reduced to drinking beer in the Black Cat."

The Treasury man took out his watch, consulted it, and muttered, "I fear you're right."

The moon was overhead now, and the whole length of the alley was clearly visible, and as clearly empty. The Treasury man called out, "Hey, Duncan? Come here a min-

4

ute, will you?" So the husky gent in the blue uniform of the Denver police got up from behind his ash can to join them. The Treasury man said, "You were at Police Head-quarters when the tip came in. Tell us about it again."

Sergeant Duncan shrugged. "It was simple enough, boys. One of the vags in the drunk tank asked the desk officer if we'd let him out for a hot tip. You know the tip. The vag said he'd heard on the street that the Careful Corrigans were recruiting help and that the job was the U. S. Mint building. He said he thought it would be tonight. But he couldn't tell us whether they meant the main mint or this substation. So now you know as much as me, and I told you all this earlier."

Longarm chewed his unlit cheroot thoughtfully. "Did you boys let the informer go?" he asked.

Duncan said, "Of course. That's the way the game is played. He was only in on a disturbance charge in the first place, and the law does favors for people who offer helpful hints."

Longarm nodded. "Yeah. He'd have known before he got himself picked up that you'd let him go once he had a little chat with the desk. I know at least a hundred Larimer Street drifters I could hire for such a task, and it wouldn't cost me more than a pocket full of drinking money, either."

Duncan asked, "Jesus, are you saying we could have been sent on a snipe hunt, Longarm? What would be the infernal point?"

"I'm still studying on that," Longarm replied. "Whatever the point was, it's got damn near every lawman in the county working overtime, all in just two places. Tell me some more about this here talkative gent in your drunk tank, Duncan. Does he have a name?"

"Sure. It was old Shep Conway," Duncan said. "He spends time in the tank regular. They say he spent some time in jail for more serious matters in his misspent youth, but his nerve's gone and he just seems to be a mean drunk, these days."

The Treasury man swore softly. "We have city, state,

and Federal law working overtime on the word of a talkative drunk?"

Duncan looked defensive and said quickly, "Hell, boys, it *sounded* like a good tip. Like I said, in his salad days, Conway spent some heavy time. He's a known associate of some real criminals. He was once a cell mate of Big Tom Corrigan, the boss of the gang we're talking about."

Longarm said, "I admire his loyalty to his old cell mates. What was this Shep Conway doing time for back then, Duncan?"

"He was a confidence man," the big policeman replied. "They say he was a pisser at conning folks in his day. Started as a shell game operator right after the War and graduated to selling gold mines and such till they caught him. But, like I said, his nerve left him in prison. Since getting out a year ago he's done nothing more than get drunk as often as possible."

Longarm nodded. "A year, huh? Big Tom Corrigan just got out this spring. Let me see your city directory, Duncan."

The policeman took out the booklet Longarm knew they all carried and handed it over. Longarm glanced up and down, saw the alley was still clear, and struck a match. Duncan asked him what he was looking for and Longarm said, "The third shell, of course."

He held the flickering match above the map in the front of the city directory. "All right, we're here betwixt Market and Blake with half the law in town either in this alley or staked out all about. The other big stakeout is a good twelve blocks away, covering the main mint. If we heard a blast coming from the east we'd think it was the main mint and head that way. If they heard a blast coming from the west, they'd think this mint annex had been hit and head for us to help. So let's see what we got in the middle and—Powder River and let her buck! I've got six city blocks to cover, quick!"

He got to his feet and started calling out to his fellow deputies from Justice. The Treasury man gasped, "What in hell are you talking about? You can't leave now. I need you!"

Longarm said, "I doubt that. But you can stay here if you've a mind to. Duncan, what about you and your coppers?"

"We're with *you*, Longarm. We know you of old. But where the hell do you mean to lead us? What did you see in that map just now?"

Longarm was already legging it down the alley with six deputies, Duncan, and a squad of Denver policemen in tow. Henry from the office hesitated. Henry was like that. But he knew Longarm of old, too, and the boss had said to find Longarm and stick with him. So Henry followed, clucking like a worried hen. The Treasury man told two of his men who started to follow to stay put.

Longarm led his followers out of the alley and up the dark, deserted street to the east. The shadows were darker on the south side of the street, so Longarm cut across, not running, but making good time in his low-heeled army boots. Duncan had shorter legs, so he had to jog at Longarm's side as he pleaded, "Can't I even have a *hint* as to where we're headed, Longarm?"

Longarm said, "The pea is under the shell in the middle. Like I said, payday's coming, and most outfits here and about pay by the month, in paper money, which is even lighter than gold."

"I know that. I'm fixing to get paid, too. But the infernal mint don't handle payrolls, Longarm!"

"Of course they don't. *Banks* do. According to your map, there's just one fair-sized bank exactly betwixt the two mint buildings. The Drovers' Trust on Champa Street. And whilst we're jawing about it, the gang's false tip has every lawman in town gathered six blocks away in both directions. Do I have to draw you a *picture*, for God's sake?"

Duncan gasped. "Lord have mercy, no! Can't we go any faster?"

Longarm shook his head. "Nope. Don't want to close

7

in all strung out. Experience has shown me there's always someone in the bunch who can't run a quarter mile."

A milk wagon, out a mite early, was overtaking them. Nobody but Longarm paid it any mind. But Longarm stepped out into the roadway and waved it down.

The white-coated driver reined in but called out, "I ain't got no milk for sale, gents."

Longarm said, "I know. You're under arrest. Murphy and Harris, cover the back!"

As the two deputies he'd ordered into action moved around to the back of the milk wagon, a shabby figure rolled over the tailgate into their arms. Murphy collared him and brought him around to where Longarm was covering the driver.

Duncan gasped. "That's Shep Conway, the man who gave us the tip!"

Longarm nodded and told the driver to get down, keeping his hands polite. Then he told Duncan, "You'd best leave two of your blues to run these rascals in. I've other fish to fry." Then he was climbing up into the milkman's seat. He gathered the reins and called out, "Everyone who's still with me had better climb aboard. Time's running out on us, boys."

Duncan snapped, "Brown, Flynn, you heard the man. Take them two to Headquarters. The rest with me!"

Longarm had the milk wagon in motion as the burly Duncan climbed up beside him, gasping. "How the hell did you know Shep Conway was hiding in this milk wagon, Longarm?" the sergeant asked.

Longarm grinned and said, "That was a fortunate surprise to me, too. I didn't know if Shep Conway was a drunken dupe of the gang or a clever rascal playing a waiting game whilst waiting for his old cell mate to get out and join up with him."

Duncan nodded. "We know now, and I could kick myself. The son of a bitch knew the law would notice ex-cons hanging about, so he threw us off by pretending to be a broken-down drunk. But why did you stop this milk wagon

8

if you didn't know the gent who set us up was aboard her?"

"I didn't know who was aboard," Longarm said, "but I knew this couldn't be a regular milk wagon making its morning run. It ain't even four o'clock yet."

"I've heard milk wagons pass this early, Longarm."

"Well, sure you have—going to *get* the milk down by the railyards. This wagon was headed the wrong way, empty. Can't you tell by the sound of its wheels when a wagon's empty, Duncan?"

"I wasn't paying attention. But I see it all now. Them two we arrested back there was on their way to pick up the loot in an innocent-looking milk wagon, right?"

"The contents of the vault at the Drovers' Trust wasn't all they wanted to sneak out of these parts. They meant to ride out themselves, disguised as the morning milk. Blowing up bank vaults attracts a certain amount of attention, even with every lawman in town a good six blocks east or west. But who looks at a pokey milk wagon clopping along early in the morning?"

They came to Curtis Street. Longarm called back, "Murphy, Harris, Blake, and Rogers. Pile out here and run down the block to cover the far end of the next alley east. Any questions?"

There were none. The grinning Federal deputies had worked with Longarm before. As they legged it away in the darkness, Longarm lit a cheroot to give them a lead as he pondered his next move. Then he nodded and clucked the horse into motion again. He told Duncan, "We'll enter the alley with the moon behind us, so this wagon will just be the black outline they're expecting. As soon as I rein in, you and the others pile out and take such cover as there is."

"Right. How close do we go, Longarm?"

"Close as they'll let us. Hang on, here's our corner."

He swung the milk wagon into the yawning blackness of the alley between Curtis and Champa. Under the third shell, the one the con man hadn't told the coppers about, lay the bank, in the middle of the block, facing east. The gang must have had a lookout watching. For as Longarm

9

and his followers barely entered the alley, the earth tingled and the night echoed to the roar of dynamite going off in somebody's basement.

Longarm clucked the spooked draft horse forward, knowing that was what he'd be doing right now if he was on the other side. A voice called out, "Hurry it up, Slim!" as a back door opened, illuminating a section of the alley and eight men coming out of the bank. Two stood tall with rifles at port arms, while the others walked bent over like Santa Claus carrying big sacks of toys. Longarm swung the wagon across the alley at an angle to block it some as he rolled out of the seat, firing at the two guards and yelling, "It's over, boys! Grab some sky, or don't, and die!"

After that, things got a mite confusing. One of the rifle toters went down sensibly with a .44-40 round in his chest. The other was gut shot and dead, but ignorant enough to get off a round and blow the stuffing out of the seat Longarm had just vacated. So Longarm shot him again. Duncan or one of his coppers blew away a rascal who dropped his sack of loot and slapped leather. Two more were running like hell for the far end of the alley, but the rest had gotten the message and were standing sheepishly with their hands in the air and the stolen money at their feet.

Henry yelled, "Some of them are getting away!"

Longarm didn't answer and a few seconds later, someone up at the far end yelled, "Freeze, mother! And I don't mean mother dear!"

Henry said, "Oh."

Duncan detailed two of his own men to check out the bank as the men Longarm had sent down to the far end herded the would-be escapees back to join everyone who was still breathing. Longarm turned to the bewildered clerk and said, "I'm glad you came along, Henry. The fun part's over, and now we get to do the infernal paperwork."

Duncan laughed. "I think I enjoy writing the charges up on a rascal more than I enjoy going down a dark alley after him. I see Big Tom over there in the doorway needs an undertaker more than he needs a trial. But, wait a minute, Longarm. Who's got the jurisdiction in this case?"

It was a good question. Longarm turned to the clerk from his office and said, "Henry, you studied law back East. Would you call what we got here city, state, or Federal?"

Henry sniffed. "I'd say it was a can of worms. Attempting to rob the U. S. Mint would have been a Federal offense, of course."

"Yeah, but that was just a ruse. What we just caught them robbing was a local bank. Can't we just give the case to Denver?"

"That's not for us to say, Longarm. I had the distinct impression the Treasury Department considered it *their* case. No matter whose case it may be, a lot of people are going to be mad as hell at you."

# Chapter 2

Longarm still couldn't see what he'd done wrong as he faced his boss, U. S. Marshal Billy Vail, in the cold gray light of dawn and the privacy of Vail's inner office. The shorter, older, and pudgier Vail stared soberly down at the papers on his desk as he tried to explain again. "Longarm, I know you thought what you done was right, but—"

"What do you mean, *thought* it was right?" Longarm cut in. "You know damn well it *was* right! I stopped a bank job in progress and put Big Tom Corrigan in his coffin whilst I was at it, damn it!"

Vail said, "I ain't finished. I know what you done. Betwixt me and you, I'm proud as Punch of you and my other deputies. But, officially and for the record, you fucked up. Justice was assisting Treasury last night. Treasury was in charge, and—"

"Billy, back up and pay attention. That threat against the

13

mint was just a ruse to draw all the law away from the intended target. The infernal Treasury agents were barking up the wrong tree, like the rest of us, and—"

"And, as I said, they were in *charge!* So *you* back up and pay attention! It's true you figured out what was really going on. It's true you got there just in time to stop it. But you did it by disobeying orders, old son. You weren't in charge at the substation stakeout. You had no right to run off with other lawmen sent there to obey such orders as the Treasury man in command might see fit to give you. He did not, repeat *not* tell you to leave your post or to take it with you. Treasury is mad as hell about what they call your dereliction of duty and usurpation of command."

Longarm grinned. "Is that what they call catching crooks these days, boss? I swear they must have gone to the same school as old Henry out front. He done all right last night, by the way. Is he in trouble too?"

Vail tried not to smile as he shook his head. "No. I told my clerk to join you. That's all he done. I can clear the others from this department who followed you by the same logic. But, Longarm, you were a naughty boy and I'm supposed to stand you in a corner."

Longarm blew smoke out his nostrils. "Shit, you can have my fool badge if it's agin the law these days to chase outlaws."

But as he took out his wallet Vail said, "Now, let's not get our bowels in an uproar until you see the corner, old son."

"Don't need to see no corner. I ain't about to stand in it. I'll allow I bent the rules. But I deny I done wrong. If I'd stayed with everyone else last night, the Careful Corrigans would have gotten away with a vault full of payroll money. You know it, I know it, and the damned Treasury knows it. They're just sore 'cause they never had anyone as smart as me working for them."

This time Vail laughed despite himself. "Longarm, this argument ain't betwixt you and me. I said I approved, unofficial, and the Denver police are pleased official enough to cite you personally for assisting their officers. That's what they call what you done—assisting. They're taking credit for saving the bank and payday, of course. But that still leaves us with an official bitch from Treasury, and the bitcher outranks me by three pay grades. So here's what we'd best do."

Longarm started to tell Vail what he could do, but it was physically impossible as well as disrespectful to elders. So he bit his tongue as the older man handed a yellow telegram across the desk to him and said, "Read that. It's the corner I'm putting you in till things quiet down some."

Longarm took the telegram and read it. Then he handed it back with a puzzled frown and said, "I know the Teaneck Kid. I arrested the son of a bitch a couple of years ago. I heard he'd escaped from Leavenworth, too. But this wire says he's been arrested again back East."

Vail made a steeple of his pudgy fingers as he leaned back in his chair. "That's for sure. He murdered the husband of a woman he'd been playing slap and tickle with. So the New York police have him in jail. I wired New York about the two guards the Teaneck Kid killed on his way out of Leavenworth, and the officials there agree it would save New York the expense of a trial if they was to hand him back to us Feds so we could hang the son of a bitch for them two killings."

Longarm pursed his lips and said, "Leavenworth's in Kansas, boss."

"I know," Vail said. "The marshal there rode in the Rangers with me. He says it's jake with him if the Colorado office picks the rascal up for him. You'll be working for both offices. I can make that official, since you know the Teaneck Kid on sight and it's established he's a crafty killer, so—"

"Hold on!" Longarm cut in. "Are you talking about sending me all the way to New York City?"

"Hell, I told you that was where they was holding the Teaneck Kid, didn't I? I got Henry typing up your travel orders and the release papers you'll need. You're to pick him up at a New York jail called the Tombs and deliver him safe and sound to Leavenworth. Deliver him, anyway. Leavenworth don't care how *sound* he arrives. By the time you wire *finito* from Kansas I'll know if it's safe for you to come on home."

Longarm snorted. "I see it, but I can't say I like it. Transporting prisoners is a mighty chickenshit chore for a deputy with my seniority, even when we're talking about a reasonable distance, which New York City ain't. Hell's bells, Billy, even if I make every connection perfect, the round trip figures to take me a week or more, right?"

Vail shook his head. "Wrong. I want you to take at least two, and I won't fuss if it's three! It's your seniority I'm trying to save, you fool! The tax-sucking son of a bitch who's leaning on me about you is making war talk about an official hearing. So I want you off somewheres I can't reach you. Naturally, you can reach me by wire at my home address. Meanwhile I'll be pulling strings of my own. If the big boo from Treasury ain't cooled off in a week or so I'll have to study on turning him into a *little* boo. But I don't like to start intradepartmental feuds if I don't have to. So you'd best go home and pack."

Longarm started to argue, but he saw the way Vail's jaw was set and, despite the older lawman's looks, Longarm knew there was an iron fist under all that lard. So he sighed and said, "Well, I could use a paid vacation, and them prissy dudes back East might be a welcome change from the uncouth folk one has to associate with out here in the wild West."

Rank had its privileges, so Marshal Billy Vail got to take a whole hour off for lunch. He sent his clerk to meet Longarm at the depot with such papers as the trip called for. Longarm couldn't think what on earth he'd need his usual gear for on this mission, so he showed up in his Sunday-go-to-meeting duds with his cross-draw rig under the frock coat and a carpet bag of possibles in his left fist. Henry met him in the waiting room, cocked an eyebrow, and asked, "Are you really going back East in that get-up, Longarm?"

Longarm frowned, "What's the matter with my get-up, damn it? I ain't wearing wooly chaps and a war bonnet, you know."

"That's about all you left out. They're going to razz you about that cowboy hat, Longarm."

Longarm shrugged and said, "Hell, that seems fair. We poke fun at gents in derbies out here. I don't have no other hat, Henry. I'll get my boots shined along the way, and I'm wearing the fool shoestring tie Billy usually makes me wear around the Federal building. Did you come down here to give me a hard time about my hat or did you bring my infernal pay, like Billy promised?"

Henry handed over the heavy manila envelope and said, "I did. You'll find your travel and expense vouchers clipped together as well. Marshal Vail asked me to remind you that you're supposed to keep tidier records. And he says if you bill the U. S. Government for any more ladies' undergarments he's going to be very cross."

As Longarm took the envelope and headed out for the platform, Henry walked in step with him, adding, "Naturally, the papers you'll need to pick up your prisoner are in there, along with a dossier on William Tweed."

Longarm started to say he'd heard Boss Tweed was dead in the first place and not the man he was after in the second. Then he nodded. "Oh, yeah, I forgot. That's what the Teaneck Kid called himself when folks asked for his real name. He sure was a sassy jasper. But why did Billy send me his yellow sheets, Henry? I ain't hunting the rascal this time. He's already been hunted and caught."

"The dossier was my idea," the clerk said. "I thought you'd like to bone up on the kind of man you'll be dealing with. The so-called Teaneck Kid has a reputation for treachery and—"

"Hell, old son, I know all about his bad habits. I learned them the hard way, *arresting* the son of a bitch. I was the

17

one warned the custodial officers to watch him like a hawk. But, as we know, at least two guards at Leavenworth didn't pay attention."

By this time they were out on the loading platform. The Chicago Flyer was waiting, ready to board, but they were still loading the mail and baggage cars down at the far end, and Longarm knew he faced a long, tedious time on his rump between here and Chicago. So he placed his carpet bag on an empty bench, saying, "You can light out if you've a mind to, Henry. I reckon I can find my way from here."

The fussy-looking clerk sniffed and said, "My orders were to see you aboard. You certainly travel light. Don't the leg irons take up most of the room in that one bag?"

Longarm frowned and growled, "Leg irons? What are you talking about? I don't hold with cruel and unusual punishments, Henry. It says in the Constitution that it's wrong."

"It's wrong to let a prisoner escape, too, and the Teaneck Kid seems to be good at that. But it's not my problem, thank God. You do have handcuffs, at least, I hope?"

Longarm nodded and patted himself on the rump. "Sure. Hooked to the back of my gun rig, as usual. But whether I'll need them on the Kid or not will be up to him. I have an advantage over most other lawmen he's dealt with in the past. It's been established that I can catch him. So I don't see why he'd try to run away from me."

Down the platform, the conductor yelled, "All aboard!" Longarm picked up his carpet bag, said farewell to the clerk, and got on board. As he found his Pullman seat he noted that the train was more crowded than he'd expected. Most of the passengers had been dumb enough to climb aboard right off, so they were already sweaty and red-faced just from sitting in the stuffy car under the noonday sun. As he passed a not-bad-looking gal seated with a boy of about eight, the kid pointed at him and said, "Look, Ma, a cowboy!" Longarm smiled, ticked the brim of his Stetson to the flustered mother, and moved on, thinking of what old Henry had said about his hat, and how little Henry knew about starting conversations on trains.

His own assigned seat was out of earshot of the mother and child, damn it. It was partways occupied, too. A man and a woman sat side by side in one of the facing plush seats. Longarm nodded, placed his bag near the window, and sat down across from them. He knew that, come bedtime, the porters would make his seat and theirs into a bottom bunk and fold the top bunk out of that slanted panel above them and the windows. He'd get the bottom bunk, he hoped. He took his tickets out of the envelope Henry had given him and, sure enough, he was in the right pew and got to sleep comfortably.

The strange couple across from him had the top bunk. He didn't see how that was going to work out. The gal looked fit to climb up there after dark. In fact, he felt a slight tingle in his britches as he contemplated the notion. She was a nice-looking little brunette, as far as he could see. She wore a veil over her face under the straw boater perched atop her pinned-up tresses, and she was staring sideways out the window, as if something interesting as hell was going on in the Burlington Yards. Nothing was, but it allowed him to explore her with his own eyes a mite better than he'd have risked if she'd been looking his way.

He couldn't explore all that much. She wore a travel duster as well as a practical hat and veil. But the figure under the gray poplin seemed to go in and out at all the right places. He realized the gal's husband or whatever he was might not cotton to his woman being explored with eyes or anything else. So Longarm took out his watch, nodded at the gent across the way, and said, "We should have left by now."

The man didn't answer. But the one-sided exchange gave Longarm a chance to stare right at him and, sure enough, he was still as fat and ugly as ever. Longarm decided he had to be the pretty little brunette's husband. No gal would choose such an awful-looking lover, and, since they were

19

sharing the top bunk, it wouldn't be seemly for him to be any other kind of relation.

The train didn't move. It was getting even stuffier and the silence had gone past awkwardness almost into open hostility as the fat man and Longarm locked eyes. Longarm knew it was a dumb kid game. But he hadn't started it, so he was damned if he'd avert his gaze first. He'd offered more than one polite opening and the fool just sat there like a puffed-up bullfrog in a rusty black suit. He had eyes sort of like a frog's, too, although the more Longarm stared into them, the surer he became that the average frog had a warmer expression.

The gal was aware of the game, Longarm could see. The veil blurred her profile, but her cheeks were blushing as she stared down a tumbleweed rolling across the yard in the bright sunlight. That gave Longarm a graceful way to look away from the frog-faced fat man without appearing to knuckle under. He said, "Well, if this train ain't fixing to start, I'd best get us some air."

He moved over by the window and started to open it. The fat man said flatly, "Leave that window alone. I want it locked."

Longarm raised an eyebrow, looked across at the woman, and asked, "Ma'am?"

She gave no sign she'd heard him. Longarm opened the window as wide as it would go.

The fat man said, "Close that window. I told you I didn't want it open, damn it!"

Longarm opened his frock coat to get at the smokes in his shirt pocket and clear his gun for action just in case the rascal was as crazy as he talked. Longarm took out a cheroot, nodded at the woman, and again asked, "Ma'am?"

She nodded slightly. The fat man, who was taking up two-thirds of the seat she shared with him, told Longarm, "Leave her alone and shut that damned window."

Longarm lit his cheroot, decided that blowing smoke in even a frog's face was sort of uncivilized, and said mildly,

20

"This window's on my side, friend. You can open yours, keep it closed, or throw rocks through it. But if we're going to be riding all the way to Chicago together, we'd best try to act more sociable. My name is Custis Long and I'm headed for New York City."

"I don't care who you are," the fat man said. "If you know what's good for you, you'll go sit somewhere else. I booked us a private Pullman compartment, here."

Longarm said, "So did I. Or, at least, my office did, and I mean to chide the rascals about it when I get back. On long trips I like to book a real compartment, like they have up at the end of the car. These fold-down neither-fish-nor-fowl deals ain't too private in the first place and in the second place, as you see, the folks sleeping topside and downside have to ride facing one another whether they like each other or not."

The fat man made a motion with one pudgy hand, like he was brushing flies away instead of words. "See here," he said, "I *tried* to book both bunks. They said it was too late. But you can't sit there, and we mean to use both bunks tonight."

Longarm laughed. "This just don't seem to be your day, Mr. Frog."

"Who are you calling a frog, damn it?"

"Ain't that your name? Well, that's what comes from making folks guess at your real one. Whoever you are, the railroad told you true. They sold *me* the bottom bunk, and that's where I mean to sleep tonight. As to where I may or may not sit whilst waiting for the sun to set over the lone prairie—"

The gal beside the fat man suddenly turned toward Longarm and pleaded, "Please don't twit him any more, sir." Her voice was filled with quiet desperation.

Longarm nodded and just stared thoughtfully at the fat man, who was leaning forward and staring at Longarm like a bullfrog about to catch a dragonfly with its tongue. All three of them flinched as the train suddenly started with a

21

jerk. Longarm waited until they were moving some and then he shut the window, saying, "The roof vents will have it fit to breathe in here directly."

Mr. Frog didn't answer. Longarm smiled at his companion and asked her, "Do you want me to see what I can do about getting you folks a mite more room, ma'am?"

She nodded mutely. Longarm smiled at the fat man and said, "There you go, old son. It's always easier to catch flies with honey than it is with vinegar. Just so it's understood I'm getting outten this seat of my own free will, I'm going to scout up the conductor and see if there's another way to skin this cat. Fighting over things that can be fixed is dumb."

As he rose, the brunette smiled up at him through her veil and said, "That's very kind of you, Mr. Long."

The fat man jabbed her with his elbow and said, "Shut up, you slut!"

Longarm's eyes blazed dangerously but he didn't see what he could do. The pretty little thing cowered away from the brute she was with. It was the fact she was *with* him that tied Longarm's hands. As an experienced peace officer, he knew all too well what trouble a man could get into by butting into a domestic situation, however ugly. So he turned away and went looking for the conductor.

As he approached where the mother riding alone with her boy sat, the infernal kid spotted him again and called out, "Howdy, cowboy." The mother told him to shush as she smiled at Longarm. He smiled back but kept going. He still had to find the fool conductor and he'd had bad luck in the past with gals traveling with kids. He wondered if she had taught her kid to start up with strangers. He knew some gals trained their dogs to start conversations with likely prospects.

He found the conductor up in the next car. As luck would have it, they knew one another from earlier trips out of Denver. The conductor had all the time in the world to punch tickets. They sat down together for a spell of jawing about the strange princess and her frog. The conductor said he hadn't gotten to them yet, so he couldn't tell Longarm too much.

Longarm said he wasn't sure he wanted to know all that much about them. But he added, "I sure would like to sleep somewhere else this evening, Gus. I got a vivid imagination."

Gus chuckled. "Yeah, it do give a man randy thoughts to see all sorts of males and she-males climbing into them Pullman bunks in the gloaming. If this gal's as pretty as you say, her ugly husband's dick will be aimed right down at you ever' time it goes off in her."

Longarm replied, "That's the least of my worries. The son of a bitch weighs at least three hundred pounds. I ain't sure Pullman builds them top bunks with rutting walruses in mind. Besides, she said she wanted her own bunk, and it's the least I can do. They seem to be married unhappy. I doubt *he* even wants to sleep with *her* any more. Like I said, he's crazy, besides fat and ugly. She must be crazy, too, or she'd never have married him. So how's about it, Gus? Do I have to sleep under two lunatics or can you get me another bunk?"

The conductor shook his head. "I know for a fact all the regular berths are booked, Longarm."

"How about irregular berths—and what in hell are we talking about?"

Gus said, "Well, you know we have private compartments at the ends of the Pullman cars."

"I do, and I'm mad as hell that my office never saw fit to hire me one."

"They couldn't have, Longarm. Every compartment was booked in advance long before your tickets were bought."

Longarm stared out at the passing scenery, which consisted of nothing but summer-killed grass at the moment. "I'm missing something, Gus. I tell you I want more privacy and comfort. You make my mouth water by reminding me of the compartments I already knew about, and then you tell me I can't have one. I thought we was friends."

Gus glanced around to make sure they weren't being

23

overheard as he explained. "This train's an express, but it stops along the line at big cities, like North Platte, Omaha, and such. Some of the folks who reserved berths and compartments will be getting on down the line, or maybe they won't, depending."

Longarm grinned and said, "That's more like it. How often does someone hire a compartment ahead and then fail to show up when the train rolls into the station?"

Gus shrugged. "Odds are ten to one against it. But there's more'n one compartment, so we generally wind up with extra space. I'll fix it up with the porters, but—uh—well, you know how they feel about doing favors for white men, for free."

Longarm nodded. "You know I tip good, or we wouldn't be having this conversation, Gus. I'll just sit sundown out in the salon car and you can give me the high sign when it's safe to sneak into an unclaimed compartment, all right?"

"Wrong. Conductors ain't supposed to make such deals. One of the porters will tip you off, if and when. It's only fair to warn you that we might strike out at North Platte. But, what the hell—you still have your original berth."

Longarm didn't answer. The conductor rose and went on down the train. Longarm stayed put and finished his smoke, staring out at the scenery some more. They were passing through some flat prairie thrown open to homesteaders now. The results were more depressing to look at than summer-killed grass and old buffalo bones. Each little sod house had a quarter section of land fenced in. Some of the poor pilgrims had even ploughed, so dust was added to their other miseries. Longarm worked for the government, but he sure couldn't understand it at times. Anyone with a lick of sense could see those nesters were just wasting their lives and a lot of fair grazing on some pencil-pusher's mistake. This far west a quarter section was a fiendish device to torture would-be homesteaders. Those lousy little spreads out there were just too big to die on and just too small to live on.

The crazy couple he'd left back in the next car were

bothering him, too. But by now Gus would have punched their tickets. So Longarm rose and drifted back. The gal traveling alone with the little kid didn't wait for the boy to sass him this time. She met his eyes and fluttered her lashes sort of bedroom. He nodded, since that was only decent, and moved on to sit across from Mr. Frog and the princess again. He noticed his carpet bag had been moved an inch or more. But, what the hell, the train might have jolted it, and there wasn't anything worth stealing in it. He nodded to the oddly mismatched pair and said, "This ain't official, but I won't be using this bunk tonight. So you folks may as well."

Mr. Frog said, "By God, that's white of you, Long. I'm sorry I acted so unfriendly before, but between the heat and all . . ."

Longarm nodded, picked up his carpet bag, and said he understood. The gal smiled up at him, sort of wistfully, but didn't say anything. She likely didn't want to be called a slut again.

Longarm tried to put them both out of his mind as he moved back to the salon car. He was as well rid of them as they doubtless felt they were of him. He knew Mr. Frog had been through his bag. That was why he'd decided to be polite. Longarm had, of course, put all the important papers and vouchers in various pockets of his frock coat by now. But he'd left the fool dossier on the Teaneck Kid, alias William Tweed, in the carpet bag.

So now Mr. Frog knew he was a lawman. So what? He wondered what Mr. Frog was. But it didn't seem important. A Federal deputy wasn't allowed to arrest folks just for being pains in the ass.

He found the salon car occupied. It seemed he wasn't the only gent aboard who'd found the scenery dull. But, again, luck was with him. The colored bartender remembered him from earlier trips on the old Burlington Line.

The bartender called out, "Your reserved stool is right over here, Marshal!"

A disgruntled-looking little gent who'd already likely

25

had enough cussed under his breath and vacated the stool. Longarm nodded his thanks and hooked a hip over the hardwood to order a beer. He'd have ordered Maryland rye, for serious drinking, but it was early. And the only thing more uncomfortable than riding a train all night sitting up was riding one sitting up and drunk.

Miles and miles went by, and the only change in the scenery outside was that it was getting dark. They were too far out on the prairie now to see the jagged saw teeth of the Front Range to the west, and since there wasn't a cloud in the sky, even the sunset was tedious. The wheels click-clacked monotonously and the less serious drinkers started drifting forward to see if there was anything worth eating in the dining car.

Longarm wasn't drinking seriously, but he wasn't really hungry, yet, and there was no saying how much time he had to kill. The friendly bartender said he could leave his carpet bag behind the bar for now. Longarm tipped an extra nickel for the next beer and asked what time they might see North Platte.

The bartender cocked his head to listen to the clacking wheels before he opined, "We're making good time, suh. We generally gets in to North Platte around ten or so."

Longarm grimaced and decided he'd wait a mite longer before he had his supper. He and the bartender had the whole car to themselves now, so the dining car figured to be crowded and it wasn't likely they'd run out of food if he waited a spell. He noticed that the train seemed to be slowing down. He couldn't see why, looking out into the gathering dusk, so he asked if there was a stop he didn't know was on this line.

The bartender laughed and said, "We're on Lost Engine Grade, suh. Going up a sneaky nine-degree climb. We'll be picking up speed again, directly. But the engines get to earn their keep on *this* stretch."

Longarm nodded, stared out the window to see what they were talking about, and couldn't see much of anything, the

26

way the lamps over the bar were reflecting in the glass. He picked up his beer and ambled back to the door to the observation platform. It didn't seem all that important to have a better look at Lost Engine Grade, but it didn't seem important just to sit there at the bar, either. He opened the sliding door and stepped out onto the platform.

The masked man climbing over the railing at him was likely more surprised than Longarm, for though he already had a dragoon .45 in his free hand, he didn't get to fire it as Longarm threw beer in his face and slapped leather.

He'd just blown the face off the one he'd caught climbing aboard without a ticket when one of the others who were loping their ponies up the track in the wake of the train put a bullet through where Longarm's head would have been had not he been so good at ducking. Longarm blew him out of his saddle, rolled away from his own muzzle flash, and peered over the railing again to see if there were any other targets within pistol range.

There weren't. Apparently the idea had been to swing aboard the slow-moving train and rob it, not to get killed.

The door behind Longarm slid open again and the bartender gasped, "Sweet Jesus, what are you shooting at out here, suh?"

Longarm started to tell him, then decided not to. The owlhoots still able to ride would be long gone by the time anyone could stop the train and do anything about their damn-fool play, and Billy Vail had said he wanted his top deputy out of sight and out of mind for a spell. So Longarm said, "I thought I spied a pack of coyotes. Might have hit at least two of the rascals."

The bartender said, "The Burlington Line don't allow hunting from the train no more, suh."

Longarm said he wouldn't do it again, and they parted neighborly as he went forward to see about his supper. He stopped between cars to reload his .44. He'd just done so and was putting it back in its holster when a woman's voice behind him gasped, "Oh, what are you doing, sir?"

He turned, smiling. It was the gal traveling with the little

27

boy. He said, "I was just checking my hardware, ma'am."

Then he ticked his hat and moved away before she could ask more fool questions. He had one or two to ask her, but he didn't. It was none of his business what she was doing back here near the salon car, was it?

He thought about it some more as he made his way to the dining car up front. She sure was coming on sort of forward for a respectable married gal, widow woman, or whatever she was. She might have been cruising up and down the other cars to see if she could find a like-minded gent to buy her supper.

He found a vacant table in the dining car and sat down as he considered the odds that she'd been looking for *him* to buy her that supper. He picked up the menu, opened it, and said, "Not hardly," with a grimace. At these outlandish prices, he'd never in this world be able to justify buying her—and her child as well—a full-course dining-car meal.

She wasn't bad looking, but he didn't like sneaky women, and it seemed mighty sneaky to cruise a train for a lonesome man without advertising in advance that the adventure figured to cost him double.

He ordered steak and potatoes and told them he didn't want the rabbit food even though the salad course came with supper at no extra cost. He was halfway through when Mr. Frog and the princess came in and took a table down at the far end. He noticed that the brunette walked funny, like she was sort of crippled up. He couldn't tell which leg was game; she limped the same on both of them. Her fat escort sat with his back to Longarm. The gal was facing his way, but not letting on if she noticed him. He wondered if that explained why she'd married up with such an ugly brute. A crippled gal might feel she had to marry any gent who asked her. It was a mite late to tell her she was wrong.

He was finishing his apple pie when, sure enough, the gal with the noisy little kid came in, escorted by a sort of morose-looking gent in a checkered suit. The kid howdied Longarm as they passed, but his mother ignored him, as if he was something too disgusting to contemplate. The gent

28

who'd gotten stuck with buying three suppers instead of two looked disgusted with himself. But that's what happened to suckers who snapped at the bait without sniffing it for hooks and, what the hell, if he was willing to feed them all the way to the end of the line she'd doubtless leave her kid in her bunk alone. The waiter sat her under a cruel lamp and she looked sort of plain as well as treacherous under all that face powder.

Longarm had a second cup of coffee to celebrate. But as he caught himself feeling a mite smug, he muttered under his breath, "Hold on, old son. If you're so smart, how come Mr. Frog gets to sleep in your bunk, with or without the princess, and Checkered Suit gets to sleep with the other gal, expensive menu or not, while you don't know where in thunder *you're* going to get to sleep. And, no matter where, it purely promises to be mighty wistful!"

# Chapter 3

By the time they rolled into North Platte Longarm was getting mighty sick of beer and he'd stopped smoking a while back. He didn't have to have a cheroot between his teeth in the salon car to inhale smoke. Some of it was even tobacco. The rest was soft coal.

His collar itched and his teeth felt gritty every time he stopped drinking for a spell, so he didn't. He was a big man and beer didn't usually get him drunk enough to matter, but he was feeling a mite lightheaded as the train came to a hissing halt. He walked back out onto the observation platform to clear the fumes and get a better look at North Platte. The late-night air tasted better than what he'd been breathing the past few hours, but there wasn't much to see. He'd once had an interesting gunfight somewhere along this stretch of track, but he couldn't quite remember where and it hardly mattered in any case, since the rascal he'd had it out with was pushing up daisies pretty far by now.

He saw a familiar figure scuttle like a crab across the platform and into the depot. It was Mr. Frog, even if he scuttled like a crab. He seemed to be headed for the Western Union office down that way. With any luck, the bastard would miss the train as it pulled out.

But no luck. The fat bastard came back from sending his wire well before the conductor yelled his warning "Boooooard!" and, to make it even worse, Mr. Frog came back to the salon car and bellied up to the bar.

Fortunately, he was out of speaking range, so, while they had to nod to one another, they didn't have to talk. Mr. Frog looked like he'd just swallowed a canary, if bullfrogs ate canaries. Longarm didn't care. The train pulled out and gathered speed. Longarm noticed that the fat man was ordering serious double shots of redeye, like a man celebrating something. Longarm stuck to his beer and in a little while a porter came up to him and whispered, "Your compartment's ready, suh."

Longarm left his stein and a dime extra on the bar and followed the porter. The Pullman berths had been made up for the night, so they walked sneaky and didn't say anything as they passed the swaying green canvas curtains. He noticed the one he'd given up to Mr. Frog and the princess had been made up, too. The curtains of the lower bunk were still open, so the gal was in the top one. That seemed only fair.

The reserved compartment someone from North Platte had failed to claim was at the end of the car. There was a little more light in the companionway beyond the regular berths, and the porter had turned up the one in Longarm's compartment. He stepped inside, saw that the bottom bunk had been made up with fresh sheets, and handed the porter a serious tip. Then he snapped his fingers and said, "Damn. I left my carpet bag behind the bar in the salon car." The porter said he'd go fetch it.

Longarm stood in the doorway gazing after him as the white-coated porter moved out of sight. Longarm nodded,

32

trimmed the lamp in his compartment, and headed after him. He came to the curtains of his old berth and looked both ways. The coast was clear. So he opened the curtains of the top bunk, whispering, "Not a sound, princess, lest *I* turn into a frog!"

She didn't listen. The naked girl chained in the top bunk managed not to scream, but gasped, "What are you doing? What's going on?"

Longarm said, "Later. I got some questions, too."

Finding that the cuffs and leg irons she had on weren't attached to anything solid, he reached across her, dumped her duds from the wall net into her naked lap, and scooped her up bodily to carry her to his own compartment.

They just made it. He'd just covered her with a sheet and got back to the door when he spied the porter coming back with his possibles. The porter looked puzzled as he handed the bag over, saying, "Did the lamp go out, suh?"

Longarm said, "No. I put it out. What time should we get into Omaha?"

"About five in the morning, suh. Does you wish to be wakened when we gets there? I thought you was goin' on to Chicago, suh."

"I am. So don't pester me about Omaha. Good night, George."

The porter left, most likely confused but convinced Longarm was alone as well as too strange to bother except for something important. Longarm locked the door and struck a match. The princess was staring wide-eyed up at him from under the edge of the sheet.

He lit the lamp. "Howdy," he began. "Before you say anything you might regret later, I'm a deputy U. S. marshal as well as Custis Long. I've transported prisoners myself, so I know how folks walk in leg irons. Old Mr. Frog likely has the keys in his pocket, but I've never met the lock I couldn't pick, given a little time and no distractions." He took out what looked like a jackknife and opened a blade as he added, "We'll start with the cuffs. You can work your hands out without exposing anything important, can't you?"

33

She gingerly did as she was told, keeping the sheet pinned across her breasts with her bare arms. He noticed they were heaving pretty good as he sat on the edge of the bunk beside her and took her cuffed wrists in hand. She licked her lips and said, "Sheriff Marcy knows you're a lawman. He peeked in your carpet bag while you were off somewhere. But he'll still kill us both if he catches us."

Longarm went to work on her cuffs. "Sheriff, huh?" he muttered. "I figured him for a bounty hunter. I don't know how on earth he ever got elected, and I don't want you to tell me where. He throws his weight around foolish for a real lawman, no matter how much of it the Lord gave him to spare. Hold still now, and. . . . There you go. Your hands are free. Mighty cheap cuffs if a gent means to leave a prisoner unguarded, female or not. Can you sit up and expose your legs without distracting me enough to make my hands shake?"

She laughed as, holding the sheet up with one hand and bracing herself with the other, she worked herself into a sitting position, then pulled the other end of the sheet as high as her knees, exposing the brutal leg irons clamped about the high-button shoes and stockings she still had on.

Longarm looked disgusted and said, as he proceeded to pick the locks, "It's small wonder he felt safe to leave you alone whilst he celebrated. This is going to take a mite longer; he has you double locked at ankle and knee. I want you to study before you answer, princess. It's important for me to know if that fat rascal trifled with you as he stripped you down."

She shook her head. "He pawed me with his grubby hands more than he really needed to, but, to be fair, he hasn't molested me since he caught up with me in Denver. Why?"

"You just blew hell out of a tried and true defense for she-male suspects, princess. Most prosecutors hate to go after a gal who allows the law took advantage of her, unless she's done something mighty serious."

She sighed. "If you must know, the charge was grand

larceny. And why do you keep calling me princess? My name is—"

Longarm placed a finger against her lips. "You were told not to distract me, damn it! I mean to call you princess 'cause it's the only name I ever mean to remember you by. I have a mighty poor memory, so I've already forgot who you said Mr. Frog might have been. I do know nobody fitting your description is on any of the *Federal* wants I've read recent. So, whatever you might or might not have done, he's acted illegal. It's unconstitutional to transport pretty young gals in leg irons. Or, if it ain't, it ought to be. There—we got just two more locks to go."

As he went to work on her other ankle, the princess stared down at him in wonder and asked, "What do you mean, he arrested me illegally? I swear I'm innocent, but I did panic, and I did run off before my trial, so—"

"Goddammit, princess, there you go distracting me again!" he cut in. "Don't tell me what you might have done or might not have done. I ain't no infernal judge. I'm a professional peace officer teaching a rascal who overstepped his authority a needed lesson. The reason I know he was transporting you illegal is because I spent the whole infernal morning at Denver Police Headquarters jawing about another case. Had any out-of-town lawman come in with extradition papers on a woman, someone would have mentioned it."

"He arrested me at the Drake Hotel. The Denver police weren't involved."

Longarm freed her ankle and went to work on the last lock clamping the shin bar to her calf, just below the knee. "There you go," he said. "Like I said, illegal. Hell, I'm a Federal officer, and they don't let *me* take anyone across a state line without paying at least a courtesy call on the local authorities. You skipped bail, right? Don't answer. I know the answer. Mr. Frog wasn't acting for the court or the county back wherever. He was looking to collect on you from your bail bondsman. That's who he wired from North Platte."

He opened the window and tossed the leg irons and cuffs outside, muttering, "That's that. I'm fixing to douse the lamp again, so don't scream. My heart is pure, but I don't want anyone to see you should I have to open the door a crack."

He rose, hung his jacket over the latch and keyhole, hung his hat on the wall, and trimmed the lamp. It was black as pitch, even with the window shade halfway up. He sat down on the bunk beside her again and lit a cheroot. "He'll be noticing your empty bunk most any minute now. With luck, he'll think you somehow got free and left the train in North Platte."

She shuddered and asked, "What if he doesn't? They say he's a killer!"

Longarm blew smoke out his nose. "I noticed he acted ornery," he said mildly. "That's likely how he got elected. It surely couldn't have been on his brains or his looks. If he suspicions you might still be aboard, he'll likely search for you some. There's no reason for him to search in here. He don't know I have this compartment in the first place and he wouldn't expect another lawman to be helping you in the second. I know *I* wouldn't. I ought to have my head examined."

She sighed and said, "I think you're very gallant, Custis."

"That's what I just said. I got one more question. Is it safe for you to get off in Omaha?"

"I think so. I ran away from . . . ah, further east."

He chuckled. "You're learning. All right, here's the plan. We'll just lie low till we're about to stop at Omaha. I'll see if it's safe for you to get off there. It ought to be. He took all your money when he arrested you in Denver, right?"

"Yes," she sighed. "I haven't a cent."

He said, "Sure you have. I'm staking you to a few bucks, and if you can't take her from there you don't deserve to be running around loose. Get away from the railroad depot and other places coppers expect to see folks on the run. Get yourself a job waiting tables or something and check into an all-she-male boarding house. Then. . . . Hell, I'd best not

36

educate you further about the Owlhoot Trail, princess. Like I said, I mean to give you a stake and a head start. That's all a pretty gal with half a brain ought to need."

She started to say something, but Longarm's ears were keener than hers. He clamped his hand over her mouth and whispered, "Be still. Mr. Frog's missed you, and he's taking it just awful!"

She stifled a moan of terror as Longarm got to his feet and started taking off his clothes. She couldn't see him, but the sounds were obvious. She whispered, "What on earth are you doing?"

"I said to be *still*, damn it!" Longarm said.

A few moments later there was a loud pounding on the door.

Longarm braced himself in case she screamed, but she'd stuffed a ball of sheet in her mouth and managed not to as he called out, "Who is it, and what in thunder do you want at this infernal hour?"

The man on the other side of the panel said, "This is Sheriff Marcy of Cook County, Illinois. Open up, Long."

Longarm took the derringer from his vest and a towel from over the corner sink as he moved to the door, muttering loudly, "It's all right, Mary Lou. I told you I was the law, too."

Then he opened the door a crack, exposing himself naked save for the towel around his waist. He had the derringer palmed in the same hand. The fat, frog-faced lawman was standing there with the porter. The porter looked worried and apologetic. Marcy looked like he was fixing to have a fit. His eyes bulged at Longarm as he said, "Let me in. I have to talk to you."

Longarm shook his head and said, "Not hardly. I got company and she's wearing even less than me right now. What's this all about, Mr. Frog?"

"God damn it, I'm the law, from Cook County!"

"Do tell? I asked polite this afternoon, and you never said you was. Before you go pushing at folks, I'd best advise you I'm the law, too."

"I know all about that. That's why I came to you for help. You know that sassy bitch I was traveling with? Well, she was my prisoner. That's why I didn't want you pestering us, and—"

"That sure answers a heap of questions about her taste in men," Longarm cut in, adding, "Wait a minute. You said *was*. Ain't she your prisoner no more?"

"No, damn it; she's escaped. I'll be damned if I know how. But you have to help me find her."

Longarm studied the shorter, albeit much broader, man soberly as he pretended to consider. Then he shook his head and said, "Not hardly. The, ah, lady with me ain't a prisoner. So I mean to shut this door afore we both catch our deaths from this draft. It's been nice jawing with you, Marcy, but . . ."

"You son of a bitch! Don't you dare slam that door in my face! You're the only other lawman on this train, and I need help!"

"Everyone needs help sooner or later. That's why it pays to treat folks decent ahead of time, Marcy. I savvy your problem, and I feel for you, but I just can't reach you. So, good hunting, you surly bastard."

Then he shut the door and called out, "Powder River and let her buck! Are you ready for some old-fashioned fun, Mary Lou?"

She didn't answer, of course, but he could tell from the strangled gasp she gave that his words unsettled her. Still holding the towel about his middle, he moved over, dropped to one knee, and whispered, "He might be listening. He knows your voice. But can you manage some moans of passion?"

She giggled like hell with the sheet gripped between her teeth, which was good enough, he supposed. He kissed the back of his own hand, loud and wet, then proceeded to bounce the bed springs under her loud enough to be heard. That made her laugh some more. But with the sheet in her mouth it came out sort of like an excited gal doing something mighty wild. He let out a soft war whoop, whispered,

38

"Moan, damn it!" and got up again as she let out a muffled banshee wail. He laughed, too, as he placed his ear to the door panel and listened for a spell. Then he came back to rejoin her, saying, "He's moved on, likely blushing. Where in hell did I leave that smoke?"

She whispered, "In the ash tray under the window. I snuffed it out. Oh, Custis, I was so frightened, but it was so *funny,* too!"

He chuckled and bent to get a fresh cheroot and a light from his shirt on the floor near the bunk. "I'm sorry if I acted sort of shocking just now, princess. But the only excuse I could give a fellow lawman for not letting him in was..."

"I understood that right away. You surely do think fast, Custis."

He struck a light. As he applied it to the tip of his fresh cheroot she gasped and said, "Oh, my God, we're both naked!"

He shook out the light and soothed, "Don't fret about it. Everybody's naked under their duds. In the dark, there's nothing to see, so what's the difference?"

She pulled the thin sheet higher as she replied, "A great deal. Don't you think we ought to put our clothes back on?"

"You can, if you want. I'd best stay this way in case that pesky rascal comes sniffing about again."

She giggled and asked, "Would that be fair? What if I have to make any naughty sounds again?"

He chuckled. "Yeah, it'd be mighty hard to keep a straight face if I was blocking the door in my birthday suit, knowing you was sitting prissy behind me in a duster, boater, and veil."

She laughed so loud he had to warn her, saying, "Easy, now. He knows your voice."

She tried to behave, broke up again, and whispered, "I've got the giggles. I can't help it. It's like trying not to laugh at a funeral!"

"It could be *our* funeral," Longarm reminded her sternly. "Or at least jail for you and some serious explaining on my part if anyone figures out you ain't Mary Lou."

She burst out laughing again as she asked, between gasps, "Who on earth is Mary Lou?"

"Beats me. The name just popped in my head. The point is, whoever Mary Lou is, you're supposed to be her. So simmer down. I'm supposed to be in here with some bawdy gal I picked up on this train. You're making it sound like you're a schoolgirl!"

"I know, but I can't help *feeling* like a silly schoolgirl playing a game," she gasped. "Oh, my God, they're coming back! We have to make them think we're really lovers, and I'm going to laugh, I know I'm going to laugh!" She sat up, letting the sheet fall away from between them as she gasped, "We'd better really *do* it, this time. I'm a terrible actress!"

So he snuffed out the cheroot he'd just lit and proceeded to mount her. As he got in position she stiffened and whispered, "Wait! I didn't know what I was saying! Oh, this is awful. What are you doing to me? Oh, yes, yes, *that's* the way the bed springs sound when you're *really* doing it!"

Longarm tortured hell out of the springs for the edification of anyone listening at the door and kissed her hard to muffle her voice as she moaned and carried on. By the time whoever it was had moved on out of earshot, neither of them wanted to stop, so they didn't. But after she'd climaxed and gone limp in his arms, the princess sighed and murmured, "Oh, whatever must you think of me?"

He said, "I think you're an actress who really knows how to throw herself into her part. You ain't bad, either."

"Don't be horrid. You know I only did it because we had to make it sound convincing! Custis, why are you still moving?"

"Do you want me to stop?"

She considered the option as her hips moved in time with his thrusts. Then she sighed. "No, I think we'd better rehearse our act some more, don't you?"

He nodded soberly. "Yeah, we wouldn't want to give the show away by going at it like a pair of tyros. But practice makes perfect, like they say, and I'm starting to get the hang of it. How about you?"

"Oh, yes, I'm starting to feel ever so much more comfortable in the role. Could you move a little faster, darling?"

She seemed willing, but no man made of mortal clay could have ridden the princess all the way to Omaha without an occasional dismounted break. It was dangerous to sleep, she kept ruining his cheroots before he could get one half-smoked, so they had more pillow conversation than Longarm had intended and, despite himself, he found himself getting sort of interested in her life of crime.

It was up for grabs whether she'd stolen the cash her employers accused her of stealing, he decided. It was established that the princess was sort of impulsive. She had a spotty work record, had just gone to work at the place accusing her, and was therefore the logical suspect. Skipping bail hadn't done wonders for her, either. As she cuddled naked against Longarm in the dark, toying with the hair on his chest or toying with him more personally to the rhythm of the clicking train wheels, she kept telling him she was innocent.

He finally said, "If you're innocent, you're dumb, princess. As a matter of fact, you were dumb to skip bail even if you stole the money. They didn't have a case agin you."

"They said they were going to lock me in a cell so deep I'd never see the sun again if I didn't return the money, but I didn't have the money, so . . ."

He patted her reassuringly and said, "Hell, saying and doing are two different things, princess. In the first place, the only evidence they had was that the money was missing and you'd been hired recent. In the second, no judge is about to sentence a first offending female to long-at-hard, even if she's convicted."

"But you say I made it worse by running away."

"That's for sure. You ain't cut out to be an owlhoot, Princess. You can't tell a sheriff from a frog and you let whatever he was pick you up in a transient hotel. Then you

41

let him carry you aboard this train in irons without yelling for the Denver police. Any real crook would have knowed better. You never saw no extradition papers, right?"

She snuggled closer. "Can we make love again? I don't know what extradition papers are and he never said he was a frog. He told me he was the sheriff of Cook County."

"Leave go my pecker and let's study on that, princess. I know he never showed you extradition papers. Did he show you a badge or anything?"

"No, dear. He just busted into my hotel room and chained my legs together. Then he made me board this train with him, and you know the rest."

Longarm studied on that for a time, but it was hard to keep a clear head with a pretty and willing gal jerking him off. So he mounted her again and didn't get back to her recent past until they'd shared another shuddering orgasm. Then, still in the saddle, he groped for one of the matches on the sill above the head of the bunk, struck a light, and had a look at the pocket watch he'd propped up there. He kissed her and said, "Time's running out on us, princess. If we mean to smuggle you off at the next stop, we'd best study on getting dressed."

"Don't you want to do it again?"

"Want to, but can't. I'm only human, and we'll be in Omaha by the time I can get it up again, dressed or not."

He could tell from the wistful pulsations on his semi-erection that she wasn't happy about the notion. So he added casually, "Of course, if you was a *sensible* gal, we could ride on all the way to Chicago like this."

"Oh, I'd like that. But they'd arrest me there, darling."

"Not if you turned yourself in. I know a lawyer in Chicago who could explain pretty good how you missed your trial because of a family emergency or something. He might even get you off, if you're telling the whole truth about not having the money on you when that bounty hunter caught up with you."

She raised her knees, locked her high-button shoes around Longarm's waist, and sighed. "I swear I never took

42

the money, and I'm afraid to get off in the dark in a strange town. But can I trust you? Are you sure this isn't a trick to hand me over to the law yourself?"

He decided he wasn't that limp, after all, but as he started moving again he felt detached enough to assure her, "I can't arrest you. Even if I wasn't Federal in the first damned place, what we're doing compromises me as an arresting officer. My legal position, right now, is that of, well, a friend of the accused. And speaking of positions, let's try it some more."

So they did. The princess came twice, but he was still working at it when the train pulled into the Omaha yards. It made Longarm feel a mite foolish, since the shade was up and, to his surprise, the Flyer had the station platform on this side, now. But there was nobody out there and it was dark in the compartment. He was fixing to come, so he just kept pounding as the train hissed to a halt. The change in rhythm did it. He fired into her and was about to withdraw and collapse when he saw something ugly scuttling down the platform outside and muttered, "I'll be damned. Virtue is its own reward."

She wriggled and said, "Don't stop."

But Longarm said, "We have to. We'd best get dressed. Mr. Frog ain't headed for the telegraph office this time. I think he's on to us. And after all the fine acting we done, too!"

Longarm was right. He'd just gotten himself glued back together and opened the window when, outside, he spied Mr. Frog coming back to the train with two other men. One of the platform lights glinted for a moment on the badge one of them was wearing on his chest.

Longarm pulled the shade, lit the lamp, and unhooked the cuffs from the back of his belt, saying, "Hold out your hands, princess."

She stared up at him in horror.

"More acting," he assured her. "No time to explain. Just keep quiet and let me do the talking. We're about to have visitors."

So, as he opened the door to Mr. Frog and the two Omaha lawmen, the princess was sitting by the window with her cuffed hands in her lap, looking mighty unhappy. Mr. Frog pointed past Longarm at her and chortled, "There she is! I *knew* the son of a bitch stole my prisoner!"

Longarm had seen fit to pin his own badge to the lapel of his tweed coat. So one of the Omaha lawmen frowned in confusion and asked the world in general, "What in hell is all this about?"

Mr. Frog said, "I told you in the station, damn it. This damn fool just tried to help my prisoner escape, and I want 'em both arrested."

Longarm waited until both of the Omaha lawmen had noted his badge and the cuffs on the gal's wrists, and exchanged thoughtful glances before he said, "I thought this rascal would have sense enough to leap off the train in the dark. But I see he didn't. So I'd be obliged if you boys would take charge of him."

The senior Omaha lawman who'd first demanded an explanation said, "Hold on. I ain't drunk and you're both speaking English, but you're confusing the hell out of me. First off, who's that handcuffed gal over yonder?"

Mr. Frog snapped, "She's my prisoner. I was taking her back to Cook County to stand trial after she skipped bail!"

Longarm shook his head. "Wrong. She's *my* prisoner, and he's yours, boys. It's true she run off in a panic before her trial, and she's sorry about that. When she learned I was a lawman headed for Chicago she surrendered herself to me. I'm taking her back to face the music, so you can forget about her. This is the rascal I want arrested!"

The commotion had attracted some attention by now. Longarm saw the conductor and porter coming along the corridor and hailed them in to join the party as the Omaha law asked, "What's the charge, Uncle Sam?"

Longarm said, "Impersonating. The prisoner tells me he claimed to be the sheriff of Cook County. He told me he was a lawman, too." He nodded out to the porter and asked, "You remember that, George?"

The porter nodded. Gus, the conductor, said, "Hold on. He told me he was too."

Mr. Frog looked sheepish as everyone stared thoughtfully at him. "Actually, I'm sort of a private detective," he said.

Before Longarm could ask why, in that case, he'd promoted himself to an elected official, one of the Omaha lawmen, who must have shared Longarm's professional distaste for bounty hunters, asked, "Can we see your license, mister?"

"Uh, license?"

"You say you're a private detective. Private detectives is licensed and bonded in some durned state or another. So, how's about it?"

"Well, to tell you the truth, I just sort of work for a bail bondsman in Chicago."

It got quiet for a time. Then one of the Omaha lawmen said softly, "You're under arrest, Marcy. Let's go."

Mr. Frog knew better than to argue. Longarm thanked Gus and the porter and shut the door, grinning. The princess laughed incredulously and asked, "Are they really going to put that awful man in jail, dear?"

He sat down beside her and unlocked the cuffs. "They have to. Impersonating is agin the law. Don't take your duds off till the train starts again."

"I can hardly wait. But how did you know he was a fake lawman?"

"He acted like one. No professional would have made so many basic mistakes, and a man toting a real badge doesn't have to bully and bluff like he done. It was pure luck he didn't even have a bounty hunting license. I was only hoping for a Mexican standoff, but we live and learn."

The train started up again. The princess asked if she could take off her duds now. Longarm trimmed the lamp and said it was safe, now, even to take off her shoes and socks.

# Chapter 4

They arrived in Chicago sort of saddlesore. Longarm took the princess to the lawyer he'd told her about and had to hang about till the lawyer said he figured he could get her off with a scolding for jumping bail, and that when she did stand trial the case would be thrown out of court on lack of evidence. But by the time Longarm and the princess had departed in a friendly way he'd missed the New York train.

He didn't let it upset him all that much. Billy Vail had said to take his time this time, so he checked into the Palmer House on State Street to get some sleep at last.

When he woke up it was dark outside and he was hungry as a bitch wolf. It was still early enough to dine downstairs, so he took a bath, shaved, put on a fresh shirt, and went down to fill the hollow in his gut.

The Palmer House restaurant was fancier than most places he was used to, but he'd been there before, so he knew that none of the high-toned help would really hit him. He took a corner table and ordered steak, potatoes, and some of the fancy rolls the Palmer House was famous for. Their mince pie was good, too, so he ordered a second slice.

As he waited, he felt restored enough to eye the other patrons. But all the good-looking gals had some rascal eating with them. He smiled crookedly at his own randy nature. He knew the sensible thing would be for him to pick up something to read and call it a day. But the night was young, he'd get plenty of rest on the long train ride ahead, and State Street was the last wild Western main drag he figured to see for a spell. Once he took the Teaneck Kid off the hands of those sissy Eastern authorities he knew he'd have to ignore such opportunities for fun as life might offer. He had no idea how you met a good sport in New York, if they had any. But Chicago was his kind of town.

Chicago was the focal point of the cattle industry, so you ran into all sorts of cowboys—and cowgals—here. He wasn't really interested in meeting cowboys, but the gals who admired the breed talked Longarm's lingo.

As he was trying to remember some addresses from the last time he'd been this far east, a gal dressed more like New York came into the place alone. She was a head-turning redhead in a black velvet dress with gathered skirts and a tight bodice her chest was trying to bust out of. She had a sort of black feather duster perched atop her red hair, with a veil blurring her face from the lips up. Longarm decided to linger over his coffee long enough to see how in thunder she figured to eat with that fish netting in the way. But he dismissed her as a possible passing ship in the night, of course. She looked too fancy even for the Palmer House.

The headwaiter steered her toward a table near by. Longarm admired her walk. He could see she rode—likely sidesaddle after hounds and such—but she had the trim hips and stride of a born rider. As she got closer, he looked away politely. But she spotted him, gasped, and came right to his table, saying, "Custis Long! What are you doing in Chicago?"

He blinked in astonishment, got quickly to his feet, and answered, "I thought you was living near Denver these days, too, Kim."

She laughed. "I was. I'm here on business." Then she sat down at his table uninvited, so Longarm sat down, too. He didn't mind being stuck for her supper, but there were other problems to consider. He waited until the waiter took her order and left them alone before he said, "I see you're still worried about your figure, unless you really like just salad, Kim. Uh, will your husband be joining us?"

She shook her head, lifting her veil and pinning it to the feather duster holding it as she said, "No. I've been widowed again. I think I'd best stop getting married, Custis. There's something about me that seems to be fatal to the men in my life. I don't have to ask if *you're* still single, of course."

He didn't answer. He'd explained to Kim Stover, long ago when the world was younger and they'd been in love, why a lawman had no business getting married. She'd said she understood, but their bittersweet last night together had scarred them both. She nodded, as if reading his thoughts, and said brightly, "Well, what brings you to the Windy City, Custis?"

"Just passing through," he said. "I have to go on to New York City. Transporting a rascal called the Teaneck Kid."

"Oh, I've heard of him. Didn't you arrest him one time for stealing cows?"

"Yep. He stole 'em off an Indian Reserve, making it Federal. But he didn't stay in prison. He killed two guards escaping from Leavenworth, so now it's murder as well."

"He sounds charming. Why do they call him the Teaneck Kid? I've never heard of a town out West called Teaneck."

Longarm shrugged. "It's in New Jersey. They don't allow much wild stuff back East, I reckon. That's likely why Luke Short, Sundance, and the other kid called Billy come out West. You ain't really *interested* in that fool outlaw, are you, Kim?"

She lowered her eyes. "No. I never have been able to hide much from you. About that time I ran out on you . . ."

He reached across the table and took her hand to shush her. "I ain't interested in that, neither. What's done is done and we were both sort of unsettled in our heads. Tell me what you're doing in Chicago."

He had to take his hand back because the waiter chose that magic moment to plop her infernal salad in front of her. Kim waited till he'd left before she picked up her fork and said, "I came to buy some he-brutes. The price of beef is up, but the folks back East are getting picky about what it cuts and chews like."

He nodded. "I heard. *I've* never had much trouble cutting longhorn beef, but I've got strong wrists. What are you breeding your herd up with, White Faces?"

"Of course. Tender or tough, they still have to survive on the high plains. I've got my eye on a prize Hereford, but they're asking too much. I could buy two less promising he-brutes for the asking price, but, damn, he's really a beautiful animal. What would you do in my place, dear?"

"Buy the good one. Your cows will be ever grateful and, what the hell, if you're willing to settle for second rate, why bother at all? You must already have all the scrub bulls you need, right?"

She picked at her salad as she said demurely, *"Bull* is not a word to use in mixed company, dear. But you always did consider me one of the boys, didn't you?"

"I thought we had how we might or might not have felt all settled, Kim," he answered soberly.

She said, "Sorry. You're right about the he-brute, too. If anyone should know the dangers of settling for a second-rate he-brute, it should be me. I'm not hungry after all. Are you?"

"Not now. I just ate."

She stared down at her messed-up but neglected salad so he couldn't see her eyes as she asked quietly, "Are we going to your room or mine?"

He hesitated. Then he said, "I ain't sure we ought to go to either, Kim. You know how I feel about you. But, no

50

offense, you do cry a lot for a cowgal in the cold gray dawn."

This time it was she who reached across the table. She took his hand and said, "I won't cry again. I've learned how little good it does. So how's about it, cowboy—Powder River and let her buck?"

Longarm spent the next few days in Chicago with Kim Stover and they even got dressed a few times to go sightseeing or take in a show. She didn't cry when he left, because he sneaked out one morning while she was still asleep to catch the New York train.

There was nobody pretty or even willing aboard the New York Express, but it didn't matter. The scenery was getting sort of interesting and trying to crowd the lifetime he might have had with Kim into less than a honeymoon had drained him pretty good.

Longarm had been birthed and reared in West-by-God-Virginia, and he'd seen other parts of the East in his war years. But he'd sort of forgotten how green things were, how small and tidy the passing farms looked, next to the country he'd just left. Even the cows they passed looked soft and sort of sissy, and he noticed folks were staring at his hat for some fool reason. There was nothing wrong with his hat save for a couple of bullet holes that hardly showed. It was a lot more sensible than half the hats he saw on other gents. Why anybody, East or West, would wear a derby or a straw boater escaped him entirely.

It was early evening when the train pulled into the New York Central Terminal. As Longarm detrained, a colored man wearing a red cap ran up and tried to take his carpet bag. Longarm said he could manage, but that it was worth a nickel if the redcap would point him toward Police Headquarters.

The redcap said it was on a street called Lafayette and said he'd best take a cab, since it was more than two miles away. Longarm didn't think that sounded far, but he didn't want to get lost, so he followed the redcap out to the cab ranks and climbed up beside the driver, saying, "I want you to take me to that police headquarters on Lafayette Street."

The driver said he knew where it was, but added, "Don't you want to sit in the back, buddy?"

Longarm said, "Nope. Can't see much from back there, and I aim to get the lay of the land in these parts. I'm a stranger here in New York."

The driver said he'd guessed as much and clucked the carriage horse into motion as Longarm leaned back, gazing about. There was so much to see it was sort of bewildering. Longarm was used to the cobblestone paving and street lamps and such. They had them in Denver these days. They had buildings just as tall, too, at least in the center of town. But as they went block after block, Longarm asked the driver, "Is it all like this? I keep expecting them four-story-high buildings to sort of thin out, but they seem to be getting thicker as we head south and—great day in the morning!— there stands a gully wumper seven stories high!"

The driver said, "Wait till we get downtown, buddy. That's where they really scrape the sky at twelve stories or more."

"Jesus, ain't this downtown?"

"Hell, no, we're almost in the country, up here in the Thirties."

Longarm could only shake his head in wonder. He was glad he hadn't tried to pick his way through this chaos on his own. Aside from the endless rows of tall buildings there seemed to be a stampede going on. More folks than he'd seen in one place since he'd left the army were milling every damned way all about. The avenue they were on was jammed with other vehicles and he had to admire the way his driver threaded through without locking wheels or running over anybody. They dodged a street car that tore out of a side street at them as his driver spat, said something dreadful about the other driver's mother, and added, "I know this ain't my business, buddy. But I can't help noticing you're wearing a gun on your hip. The coppers sort of frown on that, here."

Longarm said, "That's all right. I'm the law, too. That's why I'm going to Police Headquarters. I've got to take my hat off to your New York lawmen if they caught the man I'm after outten *this* infernal crowd! I'd hate like hell to have to try and cut a trail in New York City. Jesse James could be standing direct across the street from you and you'd never know it."

It thinned out some in a stretch the driver called "The Village" even if it looked mighty built-up for a village to Longarm. Then they worked their way through a section of cast-iron office and factory buildings before the driver reined in and said, "There's Police Headquarters across the street."

Longarm paid him, climbed down, and nearly got run down by a brewery wagon as he headed for the main entrance across the way. He went up the steps between two big green glass lanterns and when he got inside it was even more confusing. Men in street clothes and others in blue uniforms were milling about like ants from a stomped-on nest. New Yorkers all acted like they had worms and couldn't sit still, it seemed.

Longarm finally grabbed a copper at random and explained who he was and what he'd come for. The copper nodded and led him through a mess of doors where he found a portly gent sitting at a roll-top desk, drinking coffee with one hand, smoking a cigar with the other, and likely trying to figure out a chore for his feet. But he was polite enough to hear Longarm out. He even told him to have a seat, though there wasn't one. So Longarm stood while the police official rummaged through his desk, found what he was after, and said, "Here we are, Deputy Long. William Tweed, alias the Teaneck Kid. You say they sent you to pick him up?"

"Yep. You folks have him in a place called the Tombs."

The New Yorker frowned and said, "Not any more.

Could I see your badge, Deputy?"

Longarm took out his wallet as well as the papers on the Teaneck Kid and handed them over. The New York copper read them, looked Longarm up and down, and said, "Something funny's going on. According to my flimsy, you already have the prisoner in custody."

Longarm frowned. "Not hardly. I just arrived in town less than an hour ago."

The other man said, "Wait here," and dashed out of the room with surprising grace, considering. Longarm lit a cheroot. A few puffs later the first New Yorker came back with a couple of other gents wearing derby hats and gray suits they must have bought in the same place. The first one he'd spoken to said, "We're going to have to detain you long enough to wire Denver and find out if you're the real Deputy Long. Can you think of some personal data only you and your home office might know about you?"

Longarm nodded thoughtfully and said, "Sure. I can give you my mother's maiden name and such. But what's all this about?"

The three New York coppers exchanged glances. Then one of the derby wearers said, "If you're the real Custis Long, we've been taken for a buggy ride. Three days ago another gent claiming to be Deputy U. S. Marshal Custis Long showed up to claim William Tweed as a Federal prisoner. We turned Tweed over to him."

Longarm stared at him slack-jawed.

"Yeah," the man said, "let's go send some wires. If you're the real Deputy Long—and you'd be mighty stupid if you weren't—the impostor and your prisoner have a seventy-two-hour lead on us already."

It only took the New York police a couple of telegrams to verify Longarm's identity and they'd been too polite to put a possible fellow peace officer in a detention cage. So he was sitting in a ward room with one of the derby hats, sipping coffee and cursing himself, when the other derby hat came in, sat down, and said, "Well, you're the one they

54

call Longarm. I'm Detective Sergeant Mulligan, and you already know Wojensky, here. Your Uncle Billy sends his regards and says you're not to leave for home without the Teaneck Kid. *Our* captain's mad as hell, too, so me and Wojensky have been assigned to help you catch the son of a bitch and the impostor who made chumps of us all. You Feds can have the Teaneck Kid, but the other son of a bitch is ours. Agreed?"

"Let's study on that, boys," Longarm said. "The man who helped the Teaneck Kid escape was impersonating a Federal agent. That makes him a Federal criminal, too, don't it?"

Wojensky said, "Don't be greedy. And let's not hear any more loose talk about anyone *escaping* from the Tombs. We don't let prisoners escape from the Tombs. The impostor showed up with proper credentials and papers after the Justice Department wired us you were coming. Hell, you—or that other fellow—showed up *late*. The boys at the Tombs had the prisoner's release typed up and waiting. What do you want, egg in your beer?"

Mulligan nodded. "I've been meaning to ask you about that. How come it took you so long to get here?"

"I got lost. The point is, someone else got here first. Let's study on how they intercepted the wire Justice sent you—"

"Let's get back to who gets the impostor who did," Mulligan cut in. "Your slow and casual approach to cross-country travel may have given them the opportunity, but they made us look bad, too. We don't care if he made fools of us by impersonating a Federal officer or the Czar of all the Russias. He perpetrated the crime in New York City and New York City means to keep and cherish him for a very long time. You Feds can have him if and when he ever gets out. But until that time he's our prisoner."

As Longarm hesitated, Wojensky offered, "Half a loaf is better than none?"

Longarm said, "What if I say no?"

Mulligan said, "You're on your own. My partner and me

55

have been ordered to let you tag along as a courtesy to a fellow peace officer. But if you're not willing to be courteous, too, you can go to hell."

"Is it all right if I sort of look for the rascals on my own?"

"In the middle of New York? Be our guest, cowboy."

Wojensky's voice was kinder as he said, "Be reasonable, Long. You're off your beat. You could no doubt show me and Mulligan a thing or two about trailing bandits out West. But here *you're* the greenhorn."

"No argument about that point," Longarm admitted. "But do either of you know the Teaneck Kid on sight?"

They both looked uncomfortable, so he added, "I might know his sidekick, too, since most of his criminal career has took place west of the Big Muddy. I ain't being mule-headed about the jurisdiction, boys. I just don't have the authority to hand a Federal prisoner over to local law on my own. Can't we just get cracking on catching the sons of bitches and worry about whose prisoners they may be later?"

Mulligan shook his head. "We have orders, too. The captain says we split the honors or you can't tag along."

Longarm swore. "This is getting mighty tedious. Whilst we're arguing about jurisdiction, the gents we both want are running around free, laughing at us all!"

Mulligan nodded grimly and said, "You're right. Come on, Wojensky. Time for you and me to hit the street."

Longarm asked what about him, and Mulligan told him to do something that hardly seemed possible. So he didn't follow as they both marched out.

He bent to open his carpet bag and take out the dossier on the Teaneck Kid that fussy Henry, bless him, had insisted on giving him. There was something to be said for paperwork after all.

Longarm opened the folder on the ward room table and started reading. He'd known most of this stuff when he'd arrested the Kid a few years back. But he hadn't engraved the details in his memory.

The Teaneck Kid had been such a dumb and apparently

56

harmless cow thief that the case had been easier than most. As his self-given nickname indicated, the Teaneck Kid hadn't been a real cowhand going into the cattle business for himself. He'd made so many mistakes stealing that Indian beef it was pathetic. But the Teaneck Kid was back on his own range now and, like Wojensky said, cutting an outlaw's trail was different back here.

The dossier said that the little Jersey town across the Hudson had no record of anyone named Tweed being born or even living there. That didn't mean the Teaneck Kid had given his right name, of course, but Longarm decided he could pass on a trip to Teaneck for now.

The New York coppers would have wired the Jersey law by now and if the little rascal had gone home to Mother they'd pick him up any minute. Not knowing his real name, there was small reward in trying to find some honest resident of Teaneck who might know more details about him. Besides, the older cons in Leavenworth would have told the Kid that the law always looked first at an escapee's last known address.

The typed-up records gave his height as five foot ten and weight as one fifty. He had hazel eyes and dishwater hair, no distinguishing marks or features. Longarm had an open mind on that newfangled fingerprinting system the French and some of the British police were starting to use, but Leavenworth didn't hold with the notion.

Longarm squinted his eyes as he tried to picture the Teaneck Kid as he'd looked at the time of his arrest. He'd looked mighty gaudy for a cow thief. He'd had on wooly chaps in high summer, a black silk shirt, a red neckerchief, and a Texas hat big enough for a family of Indians to live in. But when Longarm dressed the Teaneck Kid in ordinary duds, he just saw a blur. The Kid had been one of them disgustingly average-looking punks. The dossier said he was apparently somewhere in his twenties. The birthday he had given was already taken, by George Washington.

Somewhere out there in the teeming multitude, Longarm had to find an average-looking young male who had to know more about New York City and the country around it than Longarm did.

Longarm wasn't totally ignorant about New York. Anyone who could read knew about Broadway, the great Central Park, the Bowery, and such. It was like knowing there were canals in Venice or that big old arch in Paris. The trouble was, Longarm had no notion in which *direction* any of the places he'd read about might be.

He read on. The dossier said that the Teaneck Kid had acted like a model prisoner at Leavenworth and gotten on well with the cons and guards alike. One night one of the guards who had him down as a repentant punk made the mistake of turning his back on the Teaneck Kid. To give the devil his due, the kid was good with a gun. He'd shot it out fair and square with the second guard, and won. After that, the details blurred as badly as the killer's features.

Longarm closed the folder and put it away. He wasn't as interested in how the rascal had escaped from Leavenworth as he was in how he'd escaped from the Tombs three days ago. So he picked up the carpet bag and headed out to see if he could cut the trail some infernal way.

As he stepped out into the corridor, a man coming his way in a police captain's uniform stopped him and asked, "Did you make a deal with my detectives, Deputy?"

Longarm said, "Their asking price was a mite steep. You could have both crooks if it was up to me alone, but it ain't. Do you have your own message center, or do you have to send your wires out to a Western Union office, Captain?"

"We have our own wires patched into the cross-country network. Why?"

"Two reasons. For one thing, I'd like to wire my boss." Before the New York copper could tell him to shove it, Longarm added, "Marshal Vail may see fit to let you have that con man who sprung the prisoner from your Tombs."

The captain nodded and said, "Message center's down this way." Then, as Longarm fell in step with him, he asked, "What's your second reason?"

Longarm made a mental note that these boys were sharp,

even if they talked sort of funny. "I know nobody from my home office wired the Kid's friends I was coming," he replied. "I can't see the Kansas office betraying me, since they wouldn't have asked us to help if they didn't want the Kid picked up, and I'm giving your men the benefit of the doubt, too."

"That's very generous of you. Whom do you suspect— Western Union?"

Longarm shook his head. "It won't work. Most of their clerks I've dealt with seemed sort of mule-headed about letting even the *law* read other folks' wires. And, while a messenger boy might be bribed or waylaid, no Western Union messenger's had his hands on wire one."

By this time they'd reached the message center. The captain led Longarm to the counter and told one of the busy police telegraphers to service him. "I'll be in my office if you want to make a deal, Long."

"What if I can't, Captain?"

"Then don't bother me. I can't stop a Federal agent from wandering around on my beat, but if you get lost, ask the Fire Department to give you the ice cream and find your Mama for you!"

As the captain walked away, Longarm found a pad and pencil stub and wrote a night letter to Billy Vail, explaining in more detail how his devotion to duty had resulted in such a hell of a mess. He knew that Marshal Vail could wind up doing some explaining, too, if he didn't catch the Teaneck Kid damned soon. The idea of having a deputy out on the road all this time had been to avoid notice in high places, not to gain their undivided attention.

Longarm knew he'd have a hard time picking up return messages in such cool surroundings, so he called out to the nearest clerk, "Is there a fair-to-middling hotel in this neck of the woods?"

The telegrapher stopped tapping on his key for a moment as he thought. "Not right in this neighborhood. You might try the Majestic on Canal Street. It's middle-clean and middle-priced."

Longarm thanked him and wrote to Billy Vail to contact him there if he was fired or if there was anything else Billy might want to tell him. As he handed the blank to the friendly clerk he saw another one beyond throwing a mess of yellow blanks into a big trash barrel in the corner. Longarm asked, "Do you throw many old telegrams away, pard?"

The clerk followed his gaze and said, with a shrug, "Sure, after they've been read. You can see how busy we are. Some of the boys just leave 'em on the counter here, after they've read them, so . . ."

"Where do you get rid of your read and discarded wires?" Longarm cut in.

The clerk frowned. "Out with the rest of the trash, of course."

"Out on the street?"

"Hell, of course out on the street. Where do you throw *your* trash—in your garden? The Police Department has its trash and coal ash hauled away by the trashman, just like everyone else in New York. I'll get this night letter off in twenty minutes or so. We're pretty busy. Are you going to wait for a reply?"

Longarm said no, thanked him, and headed out to the street. Outside, the night was warm as well as dark, and the air smelled like seaweed and horse manure. The latter smell was no mystery, for the traffic was still heavy on Lafayette Street. He knew New York was a seaport, too, but he had no notion which way the harbor might be. Come to think of it, he didn't know which way Canal Street was, either.

A sober-looking gent wearing a full beard and a stovepipe hat was about to pass him, and Longarm said, "Excuse me, stranger, but I'm new in town and . . ." But by then the New Yorker was crossing his bows, not looking at him.

Longarm looked around for a friendlier face. He didn't see any. The folks going each way all walked fast and frozen-faced, as if they didn't see each other or him. He spied a gal standing on the steps he'd just come down, and she was looking his way sort of like she'd never seen a

60

carpet bag or a Stetson hat before. But she was too far off to hail and she didn't look like the kind of gal a gent could approach on the street without getting stabbed with a hatpin. So he tried to wave down a young gent in a derby, calling out, "Excuse me, I was wondering if you . . ." but the sporty-looking dude snapped, "No!" and just kept walking.

He tried a few more times and got the same results. He thought he'd never been in such a cold, unfriendly city, and that included Dodge and a couple of Mexican towns.

The gal came down the steps toward him, and as she got closer he saw that she was a pretty little thing with light brown hair under the tam she wore. Her suit-dress was cut sort of mannish, but she filled it out very nicely, for she was pleasantly plump above and below her cinched-in waist. She smiled at him roguishly and said, "You'll never get directions around New York that way, cowboy."

"I noticed. Save for present company, you New York folks sure are cold fish," Longarm said.

"Not really. You just have to know how to approach a New Yorker. Let me show you. What is it you want?"

"I'm looking for Canal Street. Could you point me at it?"

"Sure. But I said I'd show you how to get directions around New York." She took a deep breath and yelled, "Hey! Where's Canal Street?"

At least six passers-by pointed in the same direction. One even yelled that it wasn't far.

The girl laughed and said, "See? That's all there is to it."

Longarm shook his head. "You had an unfair advantage. You're a gal."

She shook her head too and said, "You try it. Don't say 'Excuse me' or 'May I have a word with you.' Just *yell*."

Longarm grinned, feeling dumb, and yelled out, "Hey, Canal?" And, sure enough, the moody-looking cuss he'd yelled at pointed the same way the others had. Longarm laughed. "You sure have odd manners in this town, ma'am," he said to the girl.

As if to prove it, she took his free elbow. "I'll explain as we walk you to Canal. I'm headed that way, anyway. I'm Billie McArtle of the New York *Sun*, by the way."

"I'm Custis Long of the Justice Department. Are you a reporter? I ain't met many lady newspaper men—no offense meant."

"None taken. We live in changing times. At least you're willing to call me a reporter. Those damned coppers back there laugh at me every time I try to get a story out of them. Where are we going on Canal?"

He frowned. *"I'm* looking for the Majestic Hotel. I didn't know *we* was going anywhere, Miss Billie. You said it was on your way."

She laughed. "When I smell a story, *any* way is my way. But first we have to educate you about finding your way around New York. We're not as unfriendly here as most strangers think. You saw, back there, how willing everyone was to give directions, once they knew directions was all you wanted. You see, it's hard to walk more than a block in such a crowded city without being accosted by a beggar, a con man, or a queer."

"Good Lord, which of them things do you reckon they took me for?"

"It doesn't matter. New Yorkers don't wait to find out. They've heard every sob story there is, many many times. They generally start with an 'Excuse me, sir,' or a 'Pardon me.' They don't want to hear the rest of the pitch. On the other hand, we're just as willing as most people to help a harmless stranger. You just have to let us know what you want, with no beating about the bush."

He studied some on her words as they walked arm-in-arm along the crowded sidewalk. Then he nodded. "I think I see the light. I ain't had many sissies pestering me since I started shaving regular, but as I look back to when I was younger, the gents who sidled up to me with impossible suggestions did start out polite. Most card sharps and con men start innocent-sounding conversations, too. But if a man used New York manners in Dodge or even in Denver, he could sure get hit a lot."

"That may well be, but you're not in Dodge City now. When you want something in New York, just come right out and holler for it. Let people know what the hell you want."

He didn't comment on her earthy way of talking for a gal. She'd just *said* folks talked cruder here than they did in other parts. As they crossed a narrow street, Billie went on, "Never show money in New York on the street. It can be dangerous, even for a man wearing a gun. I've been meaning to ask you about that bulge that's come between us. It is a gun, isn't it?"

"Yes, and the police here can't stop me from carrying it. My Federal badge outranks any local law. I've had some tedious discussions about that in smaller towns out West, but I don't think the New York coppers will arrest me. They would have already if they didn't know they couldn't."

"Me, too. All they could do this evening was throw me out. My editor sent me to check out a lead about an escape from the Tombs. But all I got from them even shocked my shell-like ears, and I thought I'd heard all the naughty words there were by now. That's Canal ahead. We swing right when we get to the corner, and your hotel's in the middle of the block."

He stared harder than he really had to at the brighter lights ahead. It seemed ornery to cuss a pretty lady reporter, but he could see why they had. It was bad enough to feel foolish; reading about how foolish you were on the front page of the New York *Sun* would smart like hell.

It didn't work. Billie said, "You must be the Western sheriff who was coming to pick up the Teaneck Kid, right?"

"I'm a Deputy U. S. Marshal, and who told you what I might be doing here, Miss Billie?"

"Oh, not every copper on the force really hates me. I managed to worm a little out of a patrolman who's sweet on me before the captain came at us, snorting like a bull, and threw me out. So how's about it, Longarm?"

He saw she'd gotten quite a few facts indeed. "You mean to print something about it either way, right?"

"Absolutely. I'll confess I'll be working with uncon-firmed rumors I'll have to quote as 'unofficial sources,' and I mean to stick that captain with a 'No comment.' But I've enough for at least one column. Are you going to be in my story as a mean old 'No comment,' or do you want to look good?"

"What do I have to do to make myself look good?"

"Help me to make it two or more columns, of course." She saw that he didn't think much of her notion and quickly added, "Look, the Teaneck Kid didn't pull the wool over *your* eyes. You weren't the fool who released him to an impostor. See what I mean?"

"I see the captain got to that talkative young copper a mite late, and the copper ought to be ashamed of himself."

"Forget him. I won't quote him. It's not nice to get a pal in Dutch. We're talking about *you*, Longarm. If you'll give me an exclusive, I can see that the Police Department gets all the blame and you'll come out smelling like roses. What do you say? Do you want to work with me or against me?"

They came to the corner and, sure enough, there was the hotel sign amid all the others offering everything from soup to nuts as far as the eye could see. How in hell was he to begin looking for the Teaneck Kid when even one infernal street of New York was more cluttered and confusing than Dodge on a Saturday night?

"You know this town, and you look like a smart gal," Longarm said. "Too smart to lose a big story by playing me false, I hope. Would you be willing to really work with me? It'd mean sitting on leads you have till I wrap this case up right and tell you to go ahead. How do you like it so far?"

She dimpled. "You mean you'll give me an exclusive on the actual recapture of the Teaneck Kid?"

"Well, I have to find the rascal first. But that's about the size of it. Let me just check in to this hotel and get rid of this infernal luggage and we'll set down somewhere and figure out where to start looking."

She didn't answer. She seemed to be doing some thinking, too, as they walked as far as the entrance. As they went into the lobby, Billie said, "You'd better book us a double room, then. Would it be too much to ask if there was a bath?"

He stopped, stared soberly down at her. "I'm on an expense account. But I must say your notion strikes me as a mite unusual on such short notice, Miss Billie."

"Oh, pooh, we have to be practical," she said. "How are we to stick together if you spend the nights here and I sleep at my own flat in Green Point? The ferries hardly run at all at night, and we will be hunting day and night, won't we?"

"You must want this story mighty bad, Miss Billie."

"Don't be vulgar. I'm being practical about that, too. You're a man and I'm a woman, and it only stands to reason that if we spend the next few days and nights together we're going to wind up in bed anyway. So why don't we get that settled and go after the Teaneck Kid together with calm resolve?"

Longarm didn't feel very calm as he walked her to the desk and signed them in as man and wife. He'd done so many a time in the past, of course, but generally only after kissing the gal at least once. As he got a better look at Billie McArtle under the lobby lighting, he saw that she was even better looking than he'd thought. She just stood there beside him like butter wouldn't melt in her mouth as the room clerk summoned a bellhop to take them up to their hired room and bath.

As soon as they were alone upstairs, Longarm placed the carpet bag in the closet and, when he turned around, Billie was taking off her duds.

He said, "Uh, it's still mighty early, Miss Billie. Didn't you want to—well—have supper and jaw some, first?"

"You can take me out to dinner later," she replied. "I never said I was *sleepy*."

She hung her neatly folded dress over the back of the

65

chair she'd put her hat on, by the bed, and asked, "Will you get the light? I'm a bit self-conscious about my full figure."

He reached up to turn off the gas jet by the door, but not before he'd noticed she was built like an hourglass indeed, as she sat on the bed in her black lace unmentionables and corset to unroll her black silk stockings. His move should have plunged the room into darkness, but the room faced Canal Street and it was almost bright as day outside. Her soft curves looked even better in the gloaming glow of gas street illumination. She seemed to think it was dark enough to take off everything but her corset and lie back across the bed, bare feet on the carpet and knees neither coyly crossed nor inviting lewdly.

He didn't know what to say, so he just took off his own duds and climbed aboard. There was a lot to climb on, considering how short she was. Her ample rump called for no pillow under it and her big breasts cushioned his chest as he got their more important parts lined up and entered her.

She hissed in surprise. "Damn, you might have *warned* me!"

He stopped, leaving it in to let her get used to it as he grinned down at her in the ruddy light. "You told me New Yorkers like to get right to the point, Billie."

She spread her plump thighs wider, laughed, and said, "If that thing had a point, I'd be dead right now! I see now why they call you Long."

She gingerly raised her dimpled knees, braced them against Longarm's chest, and sighed. "That's better. A girl needs to keep her guard up with you, I see."

He saw a lot, too, as he started moving, with his locked elbows holding him higher than usual above her. Billie relaxed with her plump arms above her head on the mattress, eyes closed, a dreamy smile on her rosebud mouth. He grinned as he realized he'd yet to kiss her. This didn't seem to be the time or place. Her pink-nippled breasts swayed in time with his thrusts and, though he tried to hold back he couldn't help coming fast in such tight quarters. So he did, and then kept going. He owed it to them both.

He'd been thrusting as deep as her knees allowed. But as she moved her knees from his chest and opened her thighs wider he learned how much he'd been missing. She moaned and locked her ankles across his bouncing butt as this time they climaxed together. He went limp atop her and kissed her hot and heavy while she milked his shaft with the throbs of her afterglow and explored his mouth with her little pink tongue.

When they came up for air, she said, "I think I suffered internal injuries, but it was worth it."

"I think that corset's causing part of your discomfort, Billie. When a gal cinches her middle that tight, her innards have to go *some* damned place."

"I know," she said. "Remind me to take it off the next time we do this. Do you find me too fat, darling?"

He started moving in her again. "Hell, no!"

But before they could get really hot again Billie said, "Stop. We can do it some more later, but we're not going to catch the Teaneck Kid like this."

He laughed. "I'd forgotten all about him. What's our next best move, honey?"

"Not the moves you're making at the moment—but it sure feels good. Seriously, Longarm, we'd better get dressed. We'll compare notes over dinner. Once I have an idea what kind of man we're after, I'll be able to tell you better what part of town to start in."

As he started to withdraw, she wrapped her arms as well as legs around him and said, "Wait! It *is* sort of early for the street people to be up and about, but I'm afraid it's too late for me to stop!"

He started moving faster and again she flinched and said, "Damn. You're right about this corset having too much of me pushed down to meet you. Get off a minute, will you?"

He did as she asked, expecting her to unlace herself. But Billie rolled over and got onto her elbows and knees, presenting her hind end, and in that position she did look mighty plump indeed. As he took her wide hips in hand to take her that way, he saw that she knew her own anatomy and they fit just right, now. So he closed his eyes and let himself go and from the way she was moaning and dancing in time with his thrusts she was enjoying it even more.

Her surprisingly sporting attitude had worried Longarm a mite at first. He'd been afraid Billie might be a cold-hearted gal who used her femininity as a weapon on poor innocent gents like him. But whatever she was, she wasn't faking, for he'd been willing to quit, and this was *her* idea, bless her rollicking rump!

Of course, that didn't mean he had to trust her completely. *He* was thinking privately, even while he was enjoying the hell out of what they were doing, so she could have some cards close to her vest, too. But even if she was combining business with pleasure, he didn't see how she could play him false. She already had the main points of the damned story and, hell, if he wasn't about to come in her again right now, she'd likely be typing it up down at the infernal New York *Sun*. When you studied on it, he was doing his duty as a professional peace officer every time he made love to her. And it was pleasanter duty by far then some of the chores they'd saddled him with in the past.

# Chapter 5

They ate down around a corner off Canal in a Chinese noodle joint Billie knew about. It was about midnight and they were both hungry as hell. Billie said Chinatown lay just to the southeast of them, but they agreed Chinatown would be a dumb place to hunt for the Teaneck Kid. He asked what was up to the north and Billie said, "Little Italy. It's full of crooks. They say the Black Hand is run from a grocery store up on Mott Street. But you have to speak Italian to hide out in Little Italy. You don't suppose the Teaneck Kid's from Palermo, do you?"

Longarm sipped some of the tasty tea they'd got without ordering it and replied, "Not hardly. We exchanged some words when I arrested him a few years back, so I'd have noticed if he was a foreigner."

"What if he was an Italian who spoke good English?"

Longarm considered as he chewed and swallowed some

noodles. Then he said, "It's possible, but it ain't likely. I know about the Black Hand. They don't talk or act American. The Teaneck Kid did. So even if he had some Italian blood he never saw fit to mention, I'd be surprised to see him running with a gang in Little Italy. The punks he rode with out West was regular U. S. white trash."

Billie sipped her tea and said, "I follow your drift. My God, *I'm* starting to talk like you! But we know at least one member of the gang was a cut above your average punk, Longarm."

"Yeah, the rascal who got him out. Most of the kids riding with him that time were rounded up or killed at the same time. The ones who got away didn't seem smooth enough to con the guards at the Tombs."

"How do you like this idea? What if he's thrown in with a new gang of smoother New Yorkers?"

Longarm started to object. Then he said, "The ones he rode with out West were all Western punks, save for him. But who's to say who he might or might not have buddied up with in Leavenworth? You meet folks from all over in any Federal prison."

She nodded. "Yes, and they serve their time and leave a lot, too. It looks like the Kid made a deal with some con about to be released. We know he's from this part of the country, and—wait, it's so *simple!*"

"It is?"

"Of course, darling. Nobody helped the Teaneck Kid escape from Leavenworth. He did that on his own. Then he came back here and *roamed at large* for a time before he was arrested again for murder, and—"

"You're right." Longarm cut in. "We can forget about his Western associates. The little bastard recruited his own gang out West. When he come East after busting out of Leavenworth, he recruited a New York gang. I know what's north and south. What's due east and west?"

Billie thought. "Mostly factories down at the west end of Canal. The Bowery and Lower East Side, the other way."

"They got gangs on the Bowery, right?"

"Boy, do they have gangs! Who would you like to start with? The Plug Uglies, the Dead Rabbits, the Five Points Gang, the Black Joke? If *they* don't kill you, try Hell's Kitchen on the West Side. That's where the Hudson Dusters are."

He frowned. "Are you saying the Bowery ain't the only tough neighborhood in town, Billie?"

She laughed. "You have to be kidding! The Bowery's only one of our dangerous areas, and next to Hell's Kitchen it's a sissy. Manhattan Island is twelve miles long and there's an enclave of gang territory every other mile or so. Some as big as the Bowery or Hell's Kitchen and some smaller but just as nasty. Cross the river to Brooklyn and the Mudflat Boyos will beat you up just because they've never seen you before. That's if the Bronzeville Bashers don't see you first."

"What about over across the Hudson, then?"

"Let's see, there's the Jersey Devils and the Iron Triangle Boys. I don't know too much about that neck of the woods, as we say out West. I understand the Teaneck Kid made up the name to fool you, though. He's not from New Jersey."

"Oh? How do you know, Billie?"

"Talked to a guard from the Tombs, of course. They had him on ice a while. They said he didn't talk right."

"You mean you folks can tell?"

"Sure. Can't you tell I'm from Brooklyn?"

"Well, I noticed you don't talk like me—no offense. But you just sound like a regular New Yorker to me. Mayhaps a mite more educated."

"Thank you. The guard from the Tombs said the Teaneck Kid had an educated Manhattan accent. A stranger wouldn't notice it much, but a New York turnkey would never buy it for New Jersey. They talk *really* odd over there."

Longarm asked, "What about the con artist who impersonated me?"

"The guard I got to wasn't on duty at the time," Billie said. "I got a description, so don't blame the police too

71

much, dear. The con man was tall like you and even had a mustache and funny hat. I've no idea what he sounded like, but it must have been convincing."

"Well, I doubt like hell either one of 'em's about to come in here for some noodles. What if we started with this here Bowery?"

She gasped. "Are you kidding? They'll take one look at those shiny boots and reasonably neat suit and you'll be lucky if they don't kill you."

He said, "I gotta start somewhere, and the Bowery's close. Why don't you wait for me back at the hotel? I'll just drift over and see what I can see."

She reached across the table, spilling tea in the process, and gripped his hand protectively. "Don't you dare, Custis Long! You don't know what it's like over there late at night. The coppers don't even patrol the Bowery alone after dark. They walk in pairs—and why did you think they were issued those helmets? Come back with me and I'll take off my corset and even stand on my head for you. I'll show you around the Bowery in the morning, when the animals are sleeping in their dens. But it's after midnight and if you go over there alone at this hour they'll murder you!"

She argued like that all the way back to the hotel. Then she tried to take unfair advantage of him as she shucked out of her duds, sobbing about not wanting to have to identify his body when they fished it out of the river. But Longarm kissed her, told her to start without him if he wasn't back in a few hours, and headed for the East Side to see what all the fuss was about.

The Bowery was a broad avenue that had once been fashionable. But you only had to sniff the air to see why the poor folk lived on the East Side of Manhattan. The prevailing wind was from the south or west, so the cooking odors and horse-manure smell of the whole damned island blew toward the East River. More fashionable folk along Broadway and other north-south avenues to the west had gotten the city to pass ordinances against gas houses, vinegar

72

works, tanneries, soap works, and other such stinky notions in the tidier parts of town. But they had to be *some where*, and they were all on the East Side.

The Bowery was crowded despite the hour, but darker than most main drags, since every other gas lamp had been broken. Some of the doorways were illuminated but a lot of the loft buildings were closed and dark for the night. As you looked up or down, the Bowery folks moved through pools of light and darkness. Most were moving fast with that ant-like bustle of native New Yorkers, but some lounged in doorways, and others lay flat across the sidewalks, either drunk or dead. Nobody stopped to find out which. They just stepped over them and kept going.

Longarm felt sorriest for the ones sprawled in the gutter. The roadway was paved solid with horse shit in various stages of dryness. The New York Sanitary Corps swept the avenues to the west fairly regularly, but it hardly seemed fair to expect them to work where even a copper wasn't safe on the street.

Longarm stood on the corner getting his bearings as he tried to decide whether to head north or south. It looked awful either way. The side streets back the way he'd come had street lamps, but he could see that the city considered it a waste of time and glass to install them east of the Bowery. Canal Street lost itself in the dark over that way.

A small voice at his elbow asked, "Hey, mister, do you wanna fuck?"

He turned to stare soberly down at a dirty-faced little gal of nine or ten.

She wiped her nose and added, "I'll do it for two bits, mister."

He was tempted to give her a quarter. But he'd once done that in Juarez and he didn't want a mess of street urchins following him. So he just shook his head and walked away as she bawled, "Aw, your mudder sucks!"

An older, unattractive whore in a doorway called out to him as he passed, walking fast. He was beginning to see why New Yorkers moved so fast on the street. It likely shaved the odds if somebody threw a brick at you, too. He heard the rinky tink sound of a piano coming from an open doorway with a beer sign over it, so he went in to see what kind of saloons they had here.

The place was crowded and filled with smoke and the reek of unwashed humanity. He got his back to the wall as he studied on his chances of making it to the bar. Nobody paid any attention to him. They were all staring at the gal up on top of the piano. Longarm stared, too. She was naked as a jaybird as she did an Irish jig out of step with the piano music.

Longarm doubted he'd learn much in such a place, so he left. Outside a ragged boy of twelve or so fell into step with him and said, "You can't get any real sport in places like that, cowboy. Come wit' me and I'll show you a really doity show. You ever see a dame screw a Shetland pony?"

Longarm started to tell the kid to beat it. Then he thought and said, "That sounds more disgusting than interesting, pard. But I could use me a guide. I can see you know the Bowery, despite your tender years. How much do you figure your time is worth by the hour?"

The kid looked up at him suspiciously and said, "That depends."

Longarm gave him a quarter and said, "I'd like to see the sort of places your famous gangs congregate in."

The kid made the quarter vanish, but asked, "Whaddayah, crazy? You don't wanna go in no *gang* jernts, cowboy. Come on, I'll take you to Terrible Meg's and you can watch dames wrestle naked. Or if you don't like dames, what say we go to a jernt I know where the queers meet."

"I didn't come to see the sights," Longarm cut in. "If you don't know any gang joints, keep the quarter and go home to your mother. I'm looking for a real guide, not a sissy."

That did it. The boy said, "It's your funeral, cowboy. I'll show you to the Rabbits' Den, but I won't go in with you."

The kid led him across the Bowery and up a block past a man on a soap box who was proclaiming the end of the world. Then they went around a corner on a dark side street littered with uncollected trash and worse. As Longarm tried to adjust his eyes to the gloom, the kid said, "Watch your step, there's a stiff across the walk." And, sure enough, as he got close enough to get a better look at the dark form on the gritty pavement, Longarm saw that it was a dead man, missing his shoes. As they passed beyond, he asked how long the cadaver had been there, and if anyone knew who it was.

The kid shrugged. "Who knows? The bums just die. Sometimes wit' no help. That one's been there all day. They'll carry him off to Potter's Field sooner or later. Look, we're almost there. Sure you won't change your mind?"

Longarm could hear another piano now. "No. I'm looking for a gent who hangs out with some New York gang or other."

"Yeah? Well, if he's a Dead Rabbit, you'd better be a friend of his! That's the Rabbits' Den, there, with the lamp over the basement door. So this is where we part company, and don't say I didn't warn you."

Longarm nodded and crossed the rutted street as the kid crawfished back toward the lights of the Bowery. Longarm went down the sandstone cellar steps, tried the latch on the sheet-iron door, and found it wasn't locked. So he went in.

The piano in the far corner stopped like someone had hit the derby-hatted professor with a club. The basement room was twenty feet across and close to forty feet deep, with the bar running down one wall like at the Long Branch in Dodge. That was where the resemblance stopped. The cement floor, brick walls, and tin ceiling were all painted the same oxblood red. The men and women staring at him from barside or the tables toward the rear looked frightening, too. The men were duded up like racetrack touts and the gals wore more paint than anything else. A gal working behind the bar was stark naked, as far as he could see. He walked

75

over, nodded to the naked barkeep, and said he'd have a beer and a shot. She stared at him like he had two heads and asked, "Are you nuts?"

A jovial voice called out, "Give the cowboy a drink, Trixie. It's on the house. He's going to sing for us."

The naked girl shrugged and poured him a shotglass of redeye and a schooner of beer. Longarm raised the shotglass in a silent toast to the assemblage and downed it. He managed, with some effort, not to gasp as the awful stuff went down, and chased it fast with a gulp of beer. The beer wasn't bad.

The man who'd told Trixie to fix him up rose and came over to join Longarm as one of the other women grinned and said, "Oh-oh!"

The Dead Rabbit had an Irish face and a plug hat. He was heavier than Longarm but not as tall. He said, "We don't get many cowboys here. So sing us a cowboy song."

Longarm said, "I don't sing much, friend."

"Sure you do. Everybody knows cowboys sing. I just told the gang you was going to sing for your drink, and you had your damned drink. Are you trying to make a liar out of me?"

Longarm placed the beer stein on the bar, shrugged, and took a deep breath. Then he threw back his head and sang, in a loud baritone:

"Oh I am looking for the bully,
The bully of your town.
I am looking for the bully,
But your bully can't be found.
So bring me out your bully,
And I'll lay him on the ground.
For I'm looking for the bully,
The bully of this town!"

There was a round of applause when he finished, and Longarm bowed. Then something that looked like a moose in a shabby tweed suit put its plug hat on its table and stood up, saying, "I'm the bully of this town, cowboy. My name is O'Connel—Knuckles O'Connel—and would you tell us your darlin' name so we can notify your next of kin?"

By the time he'd got all that out, Knuckles O'Connel was halfway to Longarm and looking serious. The other Dead Rabbit slid off down the bar to give them room.

Longarm said, "They call me Longarm, and I never come here looking for trouble, friend."

"Sure you did," Knuckles said. "You *came* here, didn't you?" He was now close enough to swing, so he did.

Longarm blocked the roundhouse right with his left forearm and threw a right cross, putting all the steam he had into it. He landed on the tip of the bigger man's jaw and O'Connel dropped like a pole-axed steer and just lay there, smiling sort of sleepily up at the blood-red ceiling with his eyes closed.

There was a moment of stunned silence. Then chair legs began to scrape ominously as Longarm braced himself for the rush. He knew he'd been lucky, and John L. Sullivan in the flesh couldn't hope to take them all on with only his fists.

He was trying to decide whether to go for his derringer or the more serious .44 under his coat when a loud female, voice called out, "Two on one ain't Irish fun! The man floored O'Connel fair and square and that's the way I'm asking you other dacent boyos to fight him!"

Nobody answered as they stared soberly down at the unconscious man on the floor at Longarm's feet. The woman stood up. She was even taller than Longarm, and he was taller than anyone else still able to stand in the place. As she moved out into the light he saw that she was half-dressed in a low-cut red dress, and half-pretty, despite her size. Her black hair was pinned up, but her face looked to belong more on a good-looking man than on a woman. Her jaw was too big and her brows too bushy for a gal. She smiled grimly and said, "Well, I see nobody here but me has the guts to fight you one on one. But I'll bet I can lick you. They call me Dreadful Doris. You can see why."

He smiled. "No, I can't. You don't look dreadful to me, and I don't fight women, even when they ain't pretty, Miss Doris."

Somebody laughed. Dreadful Doris said, "Aw, cut your blarney and name your pleasure. Do you want to fight Queensberry or free-for-all?"

"If I have a choice, what if we just arm wrestled, Miss Doris?"

"Aw, hell, that's no fun. Nobody gets *hurt,* arm wrestling."

"Maybe so, but it's the only fair way male and she-male can find out who's the strongest. Are you afraid I'll beat you?"

Dreadful Doris said, "You're on. Clear us a table, damn it. Me and the cowboy's going to arm wrestle."

The notion seemed to amuse the Dead Rabbits. They cleared a table and formed a circle as Longarm and Dreadful Doris sat down across from each other, put their right elbows on the table, and locked hands. Longarm had expected her to tell him when it was time to start, so she caught him by surprise as she suddenly proceeded to crank his arm the way he didn't want it to go. He grunted, dug his elbow deeper into the hardwood table, and concentrated on hauling their locked hands back from the dangerous depths. He saw a flicker of surprise in her narrowed blue eyes as she realized how strong he was.

Doris was pretty strong herself. He got their hands upright, but then she set her jaw stubbornly, swung a big leg out to brace herself, and they were even. She was cheating with that leg, but he didn't say anything. He'd arm wrestled before, of course, so he knew they were evenly matched at brute strength and that the contest would be decided by sheer endurance. She was starting to sweat as they stared in each other's eyes, silently fighting like hell while their hands didn't move an inch either way.

Longarm had his free hand on the cross-draw holster under his coat, so he couldn't have it everywhere, and he felt someone's hand sneaking into his hip pocket. He grinned at Dreadful Doris, but he wasn't talking to her as he said, "You're wasting your time back there, whoever you may be. I don't carry my money in that pocket."

Dreadful Doris gritted her teeth and hissed, "Flannery, take your hands out of the poor man's pockets, you shameful thing. Where's your sense of honor?"

The would-be pickpocket said, "Aw, I was just practicing. He's got a gun on under that coat, Doris."

She tried to put more strength into her grip, hoping Longarm might be distracted as she asked, "Is that right, Longarm? Did you hit O'Connel fair with your fist when all the time you had a murtherous weapon on you?"

"Yep. It didn't seem right to gun a man who was only looking for fun," Longarm replied.

She laughed. "You're all right, cowboy. After I lick you, I'll let you live. You understand, of course, that the victor gets the spoils? You can keep your boots, but your gun and wallet stays here."

"What do I get if I lick *you*, Miss Doris?"

"That'll be the day. But I've a hundred or so in me garter if you do the impossible."

"I'd rather have the garter," Longarm grinned, and everyone but Dreadful Doris laughed. She blushed and he almost had her, for her arm moved a good three inches to her disadvantage and he was tempted to end it. But he let her crank her hand back up, resisting just enough to let her think it was all her own doing.

She laughed and said, "Hah, you'll not get me garter after all, I fear."

He smiled. "I fear it, too. For I sure admire your garter-wearing parts, ma'am, even if you are sort of cheating with that one leg."

She snorted and moved the leg in. Longarm saw that he'd made a tactical error, for without her unfair bracing, he could feel his advantage. She could, too, and her eyes widened as she realized she was about to lose.

Longarm said, "I'm getting thirsty. Could we stop and have us a beer? I can see it's going to take us all night to settle this infernal fight, so what say we take a break?"

Dreadful Doris said that sounded fine and yelled for drinks all around as they let go of each other's sweaty palms and dropped them to the table. Trixie came over with their beers and, sure enough, she wasn't wearing anything below the waist, either.

Dreadful Doris clinked steins with Longarm and they both sucked in some suds as Trixie served the others. "Oh me eyebrow, that feels good going down," Dreadful Doris said. "You sure are strong, Longarm."

"I've never met a gal as strong as you. Not a pretty one, leastways."

"Lave off your blarney. We both know it's a great cow I am." He didn't answer. As he took another sip of beer, Dreadful Doris asked, "Don't you think I'm big and ugly?"

"Well, I'd be a liar if I said you wasn't big, Miss Doris. But you sure ain't ugly. I'd describe you as a pretty and full-figured gal who runs a mite to size."

"Garn, are you flirtin' with me?"

"Sure. I'm a man, ain't I? But I'll stop if you've been spoken for."

She laughed bitterly and said, "That'll be the day. There ain't a man on the East Side who ain't *afraid* of me! Let's fight some more."

Longarm drained his stein, braced his sore arm, and they went at it again. It was getting a bit tedious for Longarm, but Dreadful Doris and the others seemed easy to entertain. He noticed some of the folks in the crowd were placing bets. Some were even on him. Knuckles O'Connel came over, looking sort of green around the gills, and asked what had happened to him and what was going on.

Dreadful Doris said, "He knocked you out, so now I'm fightin' for the honor of the Dead Rabbits. Sit down and be still."

O'Connel shoved a smaller man out of a chair and joined them, asking Longarm, "How did you do that, cowboy? Sure and the last thing I remember was throwing a grand punch at your darlin' mustache."

Longarm said, "Never lead with your right, Knuckles. No hard feelings?"

"Hell, you didn't stomp me or lift my wallet. You want to be a Dead Rabbit? We could use a bucko who fights like you."

Dreadful Doris grunted in pained effort. "Lave off the recruitin' till we see if he can lick me, O'Connel."

Knuckles said, "Hell, Doris, nobody can lick *you!*"

Longarm's arm was starting to hurt worse, but he wasn't ready to end it. He said to O'Connel, "I'll take a raincheck on joining your gang. But I come in here looking for a gent who might have wanted to join yours, or some other outfit. He says his name is Tweed and they call him the Teaneck Kid."

O'Connel looked blank. "Is he a cowboy sort, like you?"

"He might still dress Western, but he's a New Yorker." He went on to describe the Teaneck Kid.

Knuckles said, "You say he ain't big and he talks hoity-toity. Is he tough enough to get away with that on the Bowery?"

"He's shot at least three men."

"Yeah, but is he *tough?* What if it was him arm wrestling with Dreadful Doris instead of you?"

"He'd get flattened," Longarm said. "I follow your drift. He ain't stand-up tough. He acts meek and mild till he gets the drop on you with a gun."

Dreadful Doris said, "He'd never get in no real gang if he's a sneak. We don't admire sneaks. Are you ready to give up, Longarm?"

"Not hardly. But I'm willing to call it a draw—if you are."

He put more muscle into it to gently hint at the advantage he was offering her. Dreadful Doris wasn't stupid. She said, "Well, if Knuckles is willing to drop it, I'll have mercy on you. But you have to buy me and the others a round."

Longarm said that seemed only fair, since he hadn't paid for a drink yet. So they let go and laughed as someone else shouted, "All bets are off. The cowboy keeps his wallet and

Dreadful Doris keeps her virginity."

Dreadful Doris was blushing like a rose. It made her look more feminine, like a bashful giantess. Trixie brought their beers and said Longarm could pay before he left. It was nice to know he was going to be allowed to leave, but he wasn't through here yet. He clinked steins with Dreadful Doris and Knuckles O'Connel and they all drank. "About this gent I'm looking for," Longarm said as he put his stein down. "Is there some part of town where I might have better luck finding a boy who wanted to be a cowboy when he grew up?"

Dreadful Doris said, "What about Cow Town?"

"Yeah," said Knuckles thoughtfully. "Kip's Bay is where *I'd* look."

Longarm frowned. "Do you have a *Cow* Town as well as a Chinatown on Manhattan Island, Miss Doris?"

"Sure we do," she snorted. "Did you think New York steaks grew on trees? The stockyards and slaughterhouses are up on Kip's Bay."

Knuckles said, "Try the Bull's Head Tavern. That's where all the drovers hang out when they're in town. Hats like yours don't surprise people half as much up there as they do on the Bowery."

Longarm pursed his lips and nodded. He knew the Teaneck Kid wasn't a real cowhand, but the kid sure admired them and liked to act like one. "How far a walk is this Bull's Head Tavern?" he asked.

Dreadful Doris said, "You'll not want to *walk* it! It's miles up the river from here! You'll play hell hailing a cab in this part of town after midnight, too. The drivers don't like to pick up people from this darlin' neighborhood. Besides, it's fair late, even for New York, and the tap room might be closed at the Bull's Head."

"You ever been there, ma'am?"

"Do I look like a cowgirl? I only know the place by ill repute, but it's said it's more a rest stop than a saloon, so even if your Teaneck Kid is stopping there, he'd be asleep or worse at this hour."

82

Longarm considered as he sipped more beer. Her words made sense. He knew a man who'd busted out of the Tombs only seventy-two hours or so ago would hardly check in anywhere under his right name, and he'd already pushed his luck walking into strange surroundings after dark. His best bet would be to go back to the hotel and have a clearer field of fire in broad daylight, come morning. Billie would be worried sick by now, and he hadn't had her without the infernal corset on yet.

"I'll mosey up that way in the morning, then," he said. "It's sure been nice talking with all you Dead Rabbits. But I'd best pay the tab and be on my way."

He rose. Nobody threw a punch at him, so he walked over to the bar and paid the naked Trixie. She said she'd be getting off in a little while. He smiled wistfully at her and said another time. The disadvantage of her advertising all her wares was that he could see exactly what he was missing, and Billie was prettier all over.

He got outside and headed back to the Bowery, but stopped and turned when he heard footsteps following him.

It was Dreadful Doris. She said, "I'd better see you safely to the Bowery."

He offered her his arm and she took it, sort of coy. He felt a mite awkward, too. He wasn't used to strolling arm-in-arm with a woman a head taller than him.

"You could have beat me back there, you know," Doris said. "How come you let me off so easy?"

"I didn't want the others to laugh at you."

She gave a relieved sigh. "Oh, that was dacent of you. I was afraid you didn't want me garter."

He laughed. "You know better than that, Miss Doris. I'll bet your garter's a hell of a grand prize. But sometimes a man has to make sacrifices for a lady."

"First he calls me Miss and now it's lady! I'll bet you never wanted me garter at all."

Longarm had no idea on earth what he'd want with a garter big enough to fit Dreadful Doris. But he said he'd wanted it, anyway, just to cheer her up.

Dreadful Doris hauled him into an alleyway and said, "Well, I see I'll have to give it to you, for we both know you *won* it back there!"

"All right, hand her over."

Dreadful Doris giggled and said, "If you want it, you'll have to take it off me leg yourself."

There was just enough light for him to see that she was hoisting her skirts and, sure enough, her legs were as big as he'd figured. They weren't bad legs. They were downright shapely. But there sure was a *lot* of 'em!

He grinned and stepped closer to run his hand up under her skirts for his reward. He'd aimed for the outside of her thigh, but she moved so his hand was between them. He noticed as he slid his hand up higher that she wasn't wearing stockings, and her thigh made his hand tingle, for it was mighty smooth and soft, considering. He didn't find any garter, no matter how high he tried, and when he felt moist hair he said, "You don't seem to be *wearing* no garters, Miss Doris."

She wrapped her arms around him in a powerful bear hug as she purred, "Ain't I, now? I must have forgot to put them on! Is there anything *else* up there that suits your fancy?"

He hesitated, saw he was in trouble either way, and turned his hand over to treat her privates right as he replied, "This part feels right interesting, Miss Doris. But ain't this alley sort of public?"

"Don't tease me, you mean thing. I can't take you home, for me dear old mother would have a fit. She thinks I'm still a virgin."

"Oh? Well, mothers are like that."

"Stop the blarney and *do* it, you daft man! For it's *almost* a virgin I am, thanks to me reputation for being dreadful. Don't you *want* me?"

That was a good question. He'd never done it with a giantess before, and the dark alley they were in smelled awful. But on the other hand, she smelled good and he didn't know where on earth he could take her to do it right. So he heisted her skirts all the way up, unbuttoned his fly,

and, since it came out already rising to the occasion, po-
sitioned it experimentally. Wall jobs were hard on a tall
man, most times, but this wasn't most times. Dreadful Doris
was so long-legged that she was able to spread her awesome
limbs wide while only lowering her groin to the level of his.
So he just shoved and as she tilted her big pelvis, he was
in her.

She gasped. "You're man enough for me in every way,
you darlin' little thing!"

He knew what she meant as she hugged him tighter and
kissed him, bending her head down to do so. She kissed
good at both ends, but it sure felt strange for a man
Longarm's size to be cuddled like a sweet little bundle of
fluff while Dreadful Doris proceeded to do most of the
work. He didn't have to worry about hurting *her!* She was
big in every way and could have easily serviced a stud
horse. But thanks to her muscle control down there she was
able to clamp tight enough to pleasure him, and she seemed
to find him enough to work with. He'd already had Billie
that night, so it took him a spell to climax. She liked that
a lot, too. She beat him there and stopped moving. He
naturally kept going.

"Och, you *did* really fancy me then? That's lovely, darlin' Longarm! But your stamina is enough to worry a gorl.
A man as strong as yourself seems hard to please."

"You're pleasing me just fine, honey."

Longarm took charge of the situation. Dreadful Doris
had gone sort of limp in his arms and now he was bending
over her as they kissed. Her legs were even further apart
and he had to bend his own as they started pounding their
way down the brick wall behind her. He didn't know what
on earth he'd do if he had to hold all of her weight. But,
as she started getting hot again, it put resolve as well as
passion into her limbs so they started bouncing the other
way until, as they climaxed together, Longarm was standing
on his toes to thrust up fully into her.

She tried to twist his virile member off with her aston-
ishing muscles, only succeeded in ejecting him with her

spasms, and pleaded, "Have mercy, darling. I can't do it again. For sure I'm all fluttery and half-faint with the wonder of it all. I don't get to do this as often as Trixie and some of the other gorls. So I can't take any more right now."

His legs were killing him, too. "Well, I'll have mercy for now. But the next time we meet, be prepared."

"Och, we'd best not try to meet again, much as that thought pains me. I've me reputation to consider. Gang gorls ain't supposed to screw outsiders. *You're* in danger on this side of the Bowery, too. That was me main reason for wanting to walk you out of the neighborhood. Us winding up in here like this was a happy afterthought. But, alas, we're going to have to part now, and, if you know what's good for you, you won't come back."

He discovered he'd gone limp, put his tool away, and asked, "How come, Miss Doris? I thought I was getting along just fine with the Dead Rabbits."

"There's Dead Rabbits and there's Dead Rabbits. Most of the boyos think you're all right, now. But, though it shames me to say it, some of the gang can't be trusted in church. I have to get back to me low life. I'll go out to the far end of this alley and circle the block for the sake of me pure reputation. Make sure you go right over to the Bowery and don't take any cross street that ain't lit up well. Them Eyetalians over on the other side of the Bowery are terrible paple."

They kissed good night and goodbye. Longarm buttoned up and lit a smoke in the alley as Dreadful Doris vanished off into the dark. Then he eased out of the alley and headed for the brighter lights. He stopped and put one foot up on an ash can as if to tie his shoe. He wasn't wearing laced shoes, but it gave him a chance to sneak a look behind him without being obvious and, sure enough, a dark blur ducked into a doorway. He doubted it was Dreadful Doris following him.

He moved on, not looking back. There was one dark and narrow cross street ahead and then a long lonesome block of dark and shuttered buildings between him and the relative safety of the Bowery. He strolled innocently to the corner and ducked around it, flattening his back against the bricks as he drew his .44 and listened.

Sure enough, whoever was tailing him ran along the gritty walk to catch up. As he came around the corner, Longarm pistol-whipped him to the pavement, kicked him flat, and stomped on his windpipe. He owed the son of a bitch that final touch for the knife he'd dropped on his way down.

Longarm struck a match. He wasn't surprised to see it was the plug hat who'd first started up with him in the Rabbits' Den. Longarm made sure he was dead. He owed it to Dreadful Doris. No doubt the gang would blame this on a rival outfit. For if the sneak had told anyone his plans, Doris or the sporting Knuckles O'Connel would have likely objected.

# Chapter 6

Both Billie McArtle and Dreadful Doris had warned Long-arm about Little Italy. So he crossed the Bowery and ambled into the darkness to the west. There wasn't as much garbage on the walk, but he could see that the street lamps had all been busted out over here, too. Somebody had to be living in the four-story tenements on either side, for he heard occasional sounds of doors slamming, babies crying, and such. But all the windows facing the street were dark, as if they were heavily draped or maybe boarded over inside.

A block from the Bowery he saw a side street running the same way and decided to follow it back to Canal. But he'd only gone a few paces when some shadows detached themselves from the tenement walls ahead and blocked his path.

A purring voice with a slight accent said, "You seem to

be lost, signore." "I'm looking for Canal Street," Longarm said. "Can I get to it down this street, friend?"

"Not alive, signore. What are you doing on our block, eh?"

"I'm not looking for trouble, friend."

"You're already in trouble."

A woman's voice called out from an upstairs window in Italian. The leader of the shadowy gang called back in the same lingo and then told Longarm, "This is your lucky night. We're going to let it slide if you turn around and go back where you belong."

Longarm said that sounded fair, but he backed off a ways to make sure they meant to part friendly before he turned and made some tracks. Behind him, somebody laughed. He didn't let it unsettle him. Nobody but a fool got into a fight when he could avoid one.

As he got back on the Bowery and headed for Canal the safer way, a voice called out, "Longarm, what the hell are you doing at this hour in Little Italy?"

Longarm turned and saw Mulligan and Wojensky, the detectives. As they fell in with him he said, "I was just checking it out. It don't seem likely the Teaneck Kid would spend much time there if he knows his home town much."

"Any New Yorker coulda told you that," Mulligan said. "You're going to get yourself killed if you keep wandering around down here. Ready to make a deal?"

"I'll let you know when I get an answer to a night letter I sent. You boys have been checking the flophouses along the safer parts of the Bowery, huh?"

"Never mind what we've been doing. Why don't you go over to Broadway and bother people? A corpse your size will be a pain in the ass to the meat wagon crew, and they have enough work down here in the cold gray dawn."

Longarm saw that they were coming to Canal again, so he said he was headed west. Mulligan said he didn't care. The two detectives crossed the Bowery at an angle without even saying goodbye. Longarm shrugged, walked on to Canal, and turned right. A man dressed like Abe Lincoln waved a flag at him and said he wanted to talk to him about the Freemasons plotting to overthrow the Union, but Longarm just kept going without even looking at him. Longarm was getting to be a real New Yorker. It was surprising how short a time it took, once you studied on it.

Back at the hotel, Billie was asleep when he crept in. He tiptoed into the adjoining bath, closed the door, and ran a hot tub as he undressed. He lathered his genitals more than usual before sinking into the tub with a contented sigh. He felt a mite tuckered for some reason.

The door opened and Billie came in, without her corset or anything else on. The contrast between her short soft body and muscle-bound Dreadful Doris was considerable, and his fool organ grinder in the soapy water surprised Longarm by considering it. He'd been sure it was down for the night.

Billie said, "Oh, good. I was going to take a bath but I fell asleep." And she climbed in the tub with him. It was a big tub, but he had to sit up straighter to make room as she sat with her back to him, her broad, plump rump between his thighs as she started soaping her front happily.

"Did you run into anything interesting on the Bowery, dear?" she asked.

Longarm replied, "I'm pretty sure the Teaneck Kid ain't there. You were right about its being a tough neighborhood."

She moved her wet behind deeper into his lap as she laughed and said, "Well, I see you managed to keep your virtue, unless that's a gun you've got against my tailbone. Would you soap my back, honey?"

He said he'd be proud to. After he soaped her back, he pulled her closer, and as she reclined against his own soapy chest, he started soaping her front, too. She'd already lathered her belly and breasts with soap, but she didn't complain. It felt good to both of them. As he played with one soapy breast she took his other hand and ran it down her belly, saying, "Don't leave the best part dirty, dear."

So he started rubbing the soap bar up and down her slit and over her clit as he nibbled the nape of her neck.

Billie arched her back and gripped his wet erection with her soapy buttocks, purring, "Oh, can we come this way, dear?"

He said he didn't doubt *she* could.

"How do you know we can't get it in this way? Have you ever tried before?" she asked.

"No," he lied, "but you don't have to try and rub your ears together to know there's too much in the way. Why don't we get out—or at least turn over and do it right?"

But she had both hands on his hands and she began moaning, "Don't stop! I'm coming!" as she slopped water over the rim of the tub with her churning feet. He waited until she gave a long, passionate moan and went limp against him. Then he rose from the tub with her smooth, slippery body in his arms and toted her out to the bedroom.

He lowered her to the bed and got aboard to catch up with her. He'd had a busy night, but the contrast between her soft, wet, naked body and the giantess he'd just had in the alley inspired him to new heights. Billie seemed to like it, too, but in truth they were both getting past passion into just showing off.

After they climaxed together they dried off and got under the sheets. Billie snuggled up to him and dozed right off. Longarm was exhausted, but he didn't see how anyone ever got any sleep in New York. Despite the hour, the street outside was still brightly lit and rumbling to the passage of steel-rimmed drays, hired hacks, and clanging horse-drawn street cars.

He knew he'd never be able to sleep in such a din, but he must have, for the next time he opened his eyes it was broad daylight outside and Billie was up getting dressed.

She said she had to report for work at her paper, but she'd meet him back here around noon. She wanted to find out if her editor would permit her to work just with him alone on the big story about the Teaneck Kid.

Longarm didn't argue. He didn't want Billie tagging along everywhere he went, but she did know the city and

92

he sure wanted to keep her on his side, if only to prevent the *Sun* writing shocking things about dumb lawmen.

They had time to share breakfast in the hotel restaurant. Then Billie headed downtown and Longarm headed uptown. He waved down a cab and asked to be taken to Cow Town. It took forever. The morning traffic was so bad that Longarm was tempted to get out and walk. Nothing on wheels could get across New York faster than a nimble pedestrian. But, on the other hand, he didn't want to get lost. A million years later the cab stopped on First Avenue, high on a hill, and the driver said that was as close as he could get. Longarm paid him off and walked down a narrow side street as directed. The buildings on either side were crowded tenements. Meanly dressed men and women sat on the high stoops, staring hard at him as he passed. Some ragged kids were playing hopscotch. A couple were bare-ass naked, and one was a gal. But, what the hell, it was a warm day.

He got to the end of the street and saw why the driver had let him off on the avenue. A rickety flight of wooden steps ran down a bluff to the chaos below. Longarm lit a smoke and leaned on the stair rail to get his bearings. He saw that the river ran in line with the bluffs, about a pistol shot to the east. A red tugboat was hauling a lumber schooner against the considerable current.

Railroad tracks ran along the shoreline. To the south he saw coal tipples and the big tanks of a gas works. Closer to hand, the flats below were covered with stockyards and a slaughterhouse complex including a tannery, soap works, candle factory, and rendering plant, as well as a big packing plant and an ice house. The chutes and corrals were full of cows that had been delivered by rail to be turned into more useful products and, sure enough, he saw cowpokes down there that looked just like the ones out West. Most, of course, worked with their cattle goads on foot, but some were riding back and forth. He saw one gent working with a mighty fine cutting horse, convincing some critters that they really had no choice about where they aimed to end

93

their careers as beef and hide. The New York cowhands wore the same faded denims and Stetsons as the hands out West.

Longarm was glad he had on his Stetson and boots. The sun was hot and the dust down yonder looked ankle-deep as well as mucky.

As he went down the steps he saw a bull's head, either stuffed or carved, above the doorway of a building he'd taken at first for a big red barn. He got to the bottom and crossed the dusty, unpaved roadway. The stench of cows and salt water sure made an odd combination. He went into the tavern and saw that the cavernous barroom was almost empty at this hour. It looked like lots of other trail-town establishments he'd visited in the past, save for the new-fangled telephone set down at the end of the bar and the funny way the bartender talked. Longarm ordered a beer.

The bartender waited until he'd paid and then said, "You look like a copper. Are you after dat same fella dem udder coppers was asking about last night?"

"I fear I am, and I take my hat off to the police. I might have known they'd look for a crook with cow habits in Cow Town."

"Yeah, dey told us about dat Teaneck Kid. Nobody woiking around here ever hoid of him."

Longarm sipped his beer. "Well, I doubt he'd be using his real name, just now. Come to think on it, nobody knows the rascal's real name. He says it's Tweed, but somehow I think he's fibbing."

The New Yorker laughed. "Only Tweed I ever hoid of was Boss Tweed, and if you walk outside you can see duh jail on Blackwell's Island where dat udder Tweed wound up. Why do yuh suppose dis Teaneck Kid calls himself Tweed? It ain't a name dat's *popular* in New Yawk."

"He seems to enjoy being contrary," Longarm said. "He admires crooks as well as cowboys."

"Yeah? Well, Boss Tweed was duh biggest crook we ever had in New Yawk. But duh Kid ain't woiking as a cowboy around here. Like we told dem udder coppers, we know most of duh fellas in duh yards, and duh few who ain't been here long don't fit duh way he's supposed to look."

Longarm took out his pocket watch as he considered. Bartenders had been known to lie for a friend. But even if the Teaneck Kid had been in this neighborhood last night, he'd know now that the police were keeping an eye on it. There were a couple of foremen drinking and comparing tally sheets at a corner table. None of the working hands would likely drift in until the noon break. He'd agreed to meet Billie back at the hotel, so he drained his stein and put it down. He'd have a mosey around the yards and then head back to civilization.

As he headed for the door the cutting-horse rider he'd spied from the distance came in, saying with a Texas twang, "Lord, it's hot out there. But I got the critters in the slaughterhouse and...Jesus!"

Longarm nodded. "Howdy, Amarillo Joe. I'm a mite surprised to see *you* here, too."

But Amarillo Joe wasn't listening. He tore out the door like the devil incarnate was on his tail. Longarm wasn't the devil, but he was a lawman, and the law was kind of anxious to discuss a certain mail holdup in Colorado with old Amarillo Joe. So Longarm ran after him, drawing his Colt as he did so.

The owlhoot ran across and started up the steps, taking them three at a time. Longarm didn't want to fire down the residential street at the top of the bluff. He put a round in the wood above the fugitive's head and called out, "Give it up, Joe! Next round won't be aimed so polite!"

The Texan stopped, whirled, and produced a short-barreled sixgun from under his denim work jacket. They both fired at the same time, but Longarm's aim was better. Amarillo Joe folded over the bullet where his belt buckle used to be and came back down the steps even faster than he'd gone up, somersaulting all the way.

Longarm lowered the smoking muzzle of his .44 and walked over to see if Amarillo Joe had anything to say. He didn't. Longarm turned away and holstered his Colt as heads appeared over the top of the bluff and men came running from the stockyards. The bartender called out from the doorway of the tavern, "It's all right, he's a copper!"

Longarm entered the barroom again and the bartender said, "I already called duh coppers on duh telephone. Dey'll be right here."

"You'd best pour me another beer, then," Longarm said. "I can see I'll be here for a spell."

A uniformed patrolman arrived shortly, but as Longarm was explaining the corpse outside to him, Detective Wojensky came in. "I just heard about this when I reported in to Headquarters," he said. "That guy outside don't look like the Teaneck Kid's supposed to, Longarm."

Longarm said, "He's Amarillo Joe, a fair cowhand who dabbles in road agentry as a sideline. Uncle Sam has been looking for him for a couple of years now. His last Federal crime was a mail robbery out in Colorado, and he hailed from Texas. So naturally nobody thought to look for him in New York, of all places. Are you boys allowed to take rewards?"

"We're not supposed to. Why?"

"I'm not allowed to neither. I was hoping you'd see fit to relieve me of the tedious paperwork by saying it was your boys who caught up with the rascal at last."

Wojensky frowned. "Are you saying you'd let us take the credit for this?" Longarm answered, "Why not? He was in your town, wasn't he? He was wanted for everything but chicken pox, and *somebody* ought to tell the Justice Department they don't have to worry about looking for him no more. But, like I said, I hate paperwork. I'd take it neighborly if you could see your way to crediting him to your own account."

Wojensky looked thoughtfully at the uniformed patrolman before he asked, "How about it, McVail? Did we take him together, or didn't we?"

McVail grinned. "Sure and it just came back to me how the bastard resisted arrest after we both cornered him. It's

96

hard to say just whose bullet laid him low in all the dreadful confusion."

Wojensky bought a round of drinks and reported it in that way. Longarm asked if it was all right for him to leave and Wojensky said, "Sure. I'll have to tell the captain the truth, but officially you won't even be called as a witness. The captain likes to see the department look good, too. You're all right, Longarm. Where are you headed next?"

It was a good question. He still had a couple of hours to go before he had to meet Billie downtown. "I still like the notion of equestrian surroundings for the Teaneck Kid," he said. "Where else do folks ride a lot in New York City?"

"Hell, they ride all over."

"Yeah, but mostly in carriages, I've noticed. The Teaneck Kid likes to play cowboy. If he ain't here among the real New York cowboys, what's left?"

Wojensky shrugged. "I dunno. They got cows all over on Staten Island, and Long Island is still pretty rural. If you're talking about Manhattan, what about the Central Park?"

"You raise cows in the Central Park?"

"There's some farming there, and lots of sheep to keep the grass short. And it's about the only place in town you'd see anyone galloping about on a horse."

Longarm didn't think much of the notion. He wasn't totally ignorant of the huge park, for he'd seen prints showing the place. It seemed to him the rich folks who rode in the Central Park for pleasure rode all gussied-up, English style. But when he asked, it turned out the park wasn't far. And it occurred to him that a man playing cowboy there would surely stand out. So he finished his beer, walked out back to the stockyards, and asked about till he found the late Amarillo Joe's cutting horse. It was stabled with company-owned mounts but, as he'd hoped, the dead owlhoot had owned it personally, along with a nice Vadalia centerfire saddle. So the hostler allowed him to take it as evidence.

He mounted up and headed north, looking for a place to work up the bluffs. The cutting horse was a spirited roan mare and they had some discussion before getting it settled just who was in charge. Personal mounts could be like that. But it was hot for serious bucking and when she tried to lower her head and bite his foot, he just kicked her good-naturedly in the nose. So she decided she might as well see what the stranger on her back wanted. They found a goat path up the bluffs and when they got up topside a broader dirt path led through a ramshackle neighborhood of wooden shanties out to a paved cross street. He asked a colored lady wheeling a pushcart which way the Central Park might be, and she pointed west.

He crossed three main avenues and then had to work his way across some more railroad tracks running down the island. On the far side, the houses got fancier and the streets were tree-lined and almost free of horse shit, so he figured quality folk lived in these parts. He spied a little red brick armory building built like a castle, and beyond it rose trees. This had to be it. He rode in through a gate, smiled, and told the mare, "Well, fair is fair and this surely is nice."

They topped a rise with a view of a shimmering lake. There were boats and ducks on the water and from the trees on the far shore it looked like they were way out in the country. Mighty pretty country. He hadn't seen such a nice range in some time. They got more rain here than on the high plains, so the grass was green, even in high summer. He rode on. The path they followed wound about too much to be sensible, but he didn't see any other riders cutting across the grassy bends, so he figured it wasn't allowed. He and the mare were alone on this stretch of path. He could see from the tanbark and powdered horse shit that lots of folks rode here regular. But it was getting even hotter and it seemed that New York riders favored the cooler times of day. He hailed a couple of kids playing catch ball and asked them if they knew just how big this park might be, for there was more to it than he'd expected. They didn't know for sure, so he thanked them and rode on, frowning. Like everything else in New York, the infernal park was too big. And thanks to the way they'd laid it out you could only see to

98

the next bend, so you could only cover a few acres at a time with your eyes. The lay of the land was rolling and covered with big dark boulders in every direction. A man could hide out easily in such a place. He knew he couldn't cover it all in a day or even a week. Even if the Teaneck Kid was playing cowboy in the park—and there was nothing to say he was—this was beginning to look like a waste of time.

He wheeled the mare around and headed south, wondering where he was going to leave her for a spell. He wasn't about to ride all the way down to Canal Street through New York traffic on a fractious mount he didn't know.

The path led under an arched pedestrian bridge. Longarm heard a firecracker going off and glanced up. But the fool kids celebrating the Glorious Fourth a mite late weren't tossing firecrackers off that bridge, so he rode under. As he did so, another firecracker went off in the distance. A second later, a gal riding sidesaddle came tearing up the path at a dead run, looking almost as scared as the big bay gelding she was trying to control. She sat her mount well in her tan whipcord riding habit. But she'd lost her hat— if she'd wore one starting out—and her long ash-blonde hair streamed out behind her as she hauled back on her reins, getting no results.

As she tore past Longarm, he whirled his own mount and dug in his heels, yelling, "Hang on, ma'am!"

His cutting horse tried to do her duty, but the big chestnut had racehorse lines and Longarm's mount didn't. He saw they weren't about to catch the bolting chestnut in a flat-out chase. But the bigger, faster horse was dumb as well as spooked. He was used to trotting along the path. So, though he was running like hell, he was running as if he was on tracks. Longarm and the little cutting horse didn't have to follow the path, so they cut across a bend, and through a bed of flowers to try to cut the runaway off.

As they hit the path ahead of the chestnut the runaway tried to swerve past, but the spunky cutting horse was used to dealing with more sensible cows. She put herself and Longarm across the bigger brute's bows and braced her hooves. As the chestnut banged into her, the gal on the sidesaddle flew forward, still holding the reins. Longarm caught her with his free arm, deposited her safely on her feet, and grabbed the chestnut's bit to shake some sense into the critter, cussing him softly and gently as the gal cried out, "Don't hurt him. The poor thing's just high-strung!"

Longarm said, "I noticed," as he steadied her skittish mount. Before he could tell her she might be making a mistake, the gal leaped back onto the fool horse and took command again, saying, "Thank you, sir. I don't make a habit of speaking to strangers in the park, but since you may have saved me from a most embarrassing fall, I seem to be in your debt. I am Monica Van Tassel."

"Howdy. I'm Custis Long, and your mount still looks a mite wall-eyed to me."

She patted her chestnut's neck. "Yes, those urchins upset him terribly with their firecrackers. I think we'd better call it a day. After I find my hat I'll take him home to his stable, poor thing."

Longarm let go of her bridle so she could turn her foolish mount around. He fell in at her side as they both rode back the other way. She could tell him if she didn't cotton to the notion, but she seemed to find his company comforting as they rode under the bridge and around a bend between two big rocks.

He spied her little black derby in the dust ahead and said, "You'd best rein in and wait here, ma'am. I'll scout ahead for Injuns and such."

She laughed as he rode down to the hat and swung down to lift it from the path without dismounting. Nobody saw fit to toss an explosive device his way as he rode back to hand her the silly little hat.

"Thank you," she said. "You certainly sit a horse well, but I find your habit and style unusual for the Central Park."

As she pinned her hat back onto her blonde head, he said, "Well, folks would laugh at you if this was the High Plains—and if this was Mongolia they'd likely laugh at both of us."

100

She dimpled. "You're right, of course. I didn't mean to be unkind. I merely meant I'd never met a cowboy on this path before."

"You still ain't, ma'am. I used to herd cows, but now I'm working for the Justice Department as a deputy marshal. I thank you for telling me you ain't seen any other rider dressed cow in these parts. I was just fixing to ask you if you had."

She looked incredulous. "My word, have you been searching for a Western desperado in the Central Park of New York City?"

He nodded. "I'd just decided it was silly, too. I have to get down to Canal Street without this cutting horse. Did you say something about a stable near here, ma'am?"

"Yes. Mine. Of course, we have a carriage house and stable attached to our town house over on Fifth Avenue."

"Oh, I was looking for something more open to the general public."

She smiled. "You're welcome to leave your mount in my stable, Deputy Long. It's only a short way, and you can catch a cab or an omnibus right out front on the avenue."

He said he'd take her up on that. So they rode out of the park together and, sure enough, when they came to her imposing-looking mansion taking up one whole end of a block across from the park, there was a layout attached to the back bigger than many a town livery he'd seen out West. A colored groom ran out to grab her reins as she gracefully dismounted and told him to take care of Longarm's mount, too. He noticed she talked nice to the groom, so he decided she was a good little gal, despite her fancy ways. She asked him if he'd like to come in and have some tea before he left. He said he couldn't tarry, since he was already fixing to be late. He didn't tell her he was meeting another gal. It was none of her business. She said he could come to the front door when he returned for the cutting horse.

# Chapter 7

Longarm went back across Fifth Avenue and waved down a horse-drawn cab. He'd figured it would take some time to get all the way down to Canal Street again, but it took even longer. It was almost one by the time he got back to the Majestic. He unlocked the door of his hired room, braced for a scolding, but Billie wasn't there. She'd left a note atop a newspaper on the fresh-made bed. The note said she'd arrived early and couldn't wait, as her editor was sending her to cover a big fire. So she wouldn't know he'd been late getting back himself, and she said she was looking forward to joining him that evening for supper and other pleasures. He grinned and set her note aside. But he scowled when he saw the newspaper column she'd outlined in blue pencil.

The fool she-male had published a signed article about *him*. She even gave his name. She'd not mentioned the escape from the Tombs, just like she'd promised, but she said he was a well-known Western lawman on the trail of a dangerous fugitive hiding out in New York City. She didn't say it was the Teaneck Kid, so he didn't think she'd done much damage, but it riled him just the same. Billy Vail had sent him East to sort of *lose* himself for a spell, and here he was on the front page of the New York *Sun!*

He saw no profit in hanging about the hotel, so he locked up and went back downstairs. As he was passing through the lobby again the clerk hailed him over to the desk and said, "There was a gentleman looking for you a little while ago, Mr. Long."

Longarm frowned thoughtfully. Save for Billie, no one but his boss out in Denver knew where he was staying. He asked who the gent was, and the clerk said, "He didn't leave a name, sir. He said he was with the police and asked if you were registered here. When I said you were, but were out at the moment, he said he'd meet you later at Police Headquarters."

"That sounds fair. Have I gotten any wires or other messages yet?"

The room clerk said he hadn't, so Longarm thanked him and went out to find some grub. He found a saloon with a free lunch and combined business with pleasure by inhaling some beer with the cold meats and potato salad while he studied on who might have been looking for him at the Majestic.

Billy Vail would have gotten his night letter by now, but old Billy was careful with the taxpayers' money and only wired back when he had important things to say. No news was good news from Denver. The gent checking hotel registers was likely local law, like he said.

He finished stuffing his face and went back out to take a stroll to Police Headquarters and find out what they wanted. He passed another hotel, went inside, flashed his badge at the clerk, and asked if anyone had been there looking for him.

The clerk nodded. "It's funny you should ask. There was a man in here asking about a Custis Long, just a little while ago. I told him you weren't registered here."

"What did he look like?"

"Let's see . . . He was about your height and build. As a matter of fact, he looked something like you. I could see by his hat he was from out of town."

"But he said he was a New York copper?"

"No. He said he was with some sheriff's department out West. Kansas, I think."

Longarm thanked him and left, pondering. Leavenworth was in Kansas. If things had worked out better he'd have been on his way there with the Teaneck Kid about now. Maybe the anxious Leavenworth officials were checking up on him. But wait—Leavenworth prison was Federal. The clerk had likely got it wrong. Lots of folk mixed lawmen up and thought everyone who wore a badge out West was a sheriff.

This time he didn't feel so lost in the maze of Police Headquarters. He scouted up the watch commander and asked who might be looking for him. The New York copper had no idea. None of the detectives working on the case had mentioned ever wanting to see Longarm on their beat again, and no other lawman of any description had seen fit to pay them a call since the last time he'd been there. Longarm said, "That's sort of curious. It's considered polite for a traveling lawman to pay a courtesy call on the local law before he does anything."

The watch commander nodded. "It usually saves a lot of unpleasant accidents. I'll make a note that there's another cowboy wandering the sidewalks of New York. You say he's from Kansas?"

"Nope. *He* said he was from Kansas. I don't see why the sheriff of Leavenworth County would send a deputy here, and I'd have heard if another Federal agent was being sent to back my play. Let's try her another way. Do you allow private detectives in New York City?"

The watch commander grimaced. "Unfortunately, we have to, if they're licensed and bonded. But why would a bounty hunter be after you?"

"Looking to collect his bounty, most likely. In addition to stealing Indian beef, the Teaneck Kid and his gang were said to be careless with their running irons and other folks' cows. So whilst it ain't Federal or mayhaps exactly legal, the Cattlemen's Association has a 'Dead or Alive' out on the rascal. It looks like a carrion crow might want to pester me about cutting him in on the capture. We don't get paid all that much and some Federal deputies have been known to make a deal about reward money. He might not know me as well as my friends."

The watch commander said, "I heard, unofficially, about the grand favor you did for our lads this morning up on Kip's Bay. This is unofficial, too, but I can let you look through our list of licensed detective agencies."

Longarm shook his head. "This gent don't seem to be a New Yorker. He's likely licensed by some other state. Besides, if he's looking for me, I don't have to look for him. Sooner or later he'll sidle up to me and offer me his deal." He took out his watch and added, "I got more than four hours to kill before I have to meet someone for supper. I know the Teaneck Kid ain't on the Lower East Side or hiding out in Little Italy. He ain't been seen around Cow Town and I just had a ride through the Central Park. How do I get to Hell's Kitchen?"

"You don't, if you know what's good for you," the policeman replied. "I'm sorry, but I can't assign a foot patrol to guard you up there, and it's suicide for a stranger to enter Hell's Kitchen alone."

Longarm shrugged. "I noticed it had an ugly name. What's so hellish about Hell's Kitchen, and where's it at?"

"They call it Hell's Kitchen because the Devil brews all kinds of hell in the slums along the railroad tracks and the waterfront up there. It's up in the Forties, between Ninth Avenue and the Hudson. You won't get killed in broad daylight on Ninth Avenue. But Tenth is awful, day or night.

106

The Hudson Dusters think it's amusing to toss people onto the train tracks running through their neighborhood."

"I've heard the Hudson Dusters are a mite uncouth. Tell me more about 'em."

The watch commander shrugged. "I wish I could. If we knew some of their proper names and addresses we'd have them in jail, where they belong. The Hudson Dusters are river pirates, pimps, extortionists, stick-up men or just plain bully boys, depending on mood or opportunity. They control vice and shake down the produce markets along Ninth Avenue for pocket money between other more serious crimes. At least once a week they raid a warehouse, pirate a ship in the harbor, or murder somebody important for hire. The killings that take place right in the Kitchen are just for practice, so we don't pay much attention to it. Most of their victims are their own kind, anyway."

Longarm withheld comment as he thanked the watch commander and went out to catch another northbound cab. He knew that lots of lawmen, East and West, shared the view that murdering unimportant folk didn't count. He knew many police departments didn't bother to investigate killings in the colored quarter, Mex Town, or wherever the underclass might live. But Longarm didn't see it that way. He suspected it hurt just as much to die no matter who you were. It was sloppy police work, too. It was easy to ignore the lives and deaths of outcasts dwelling in a festering slum. But, as any housewife knew, if you failed to clean in the cracks, the whole house could get infested with vermin.

The cab driver was a good sport about taking him as far as Paddy's Market at Forty-First Street and Eighth Avenue, but he said he had a wife and family and refused to go any further west. So Longarm paid up and got out.

Paddy's Market was open-air and took up a whole city block. The crowd was shabby, pushy, and noisy, but he knew he was still in the sissy parts of town, so he bulled his way west. Ninth Avenue was lined with fruit and vegetable shops, open to the avenue with the produce spread out across the crowded walk. He noticed a lot of the folks jabbered in foreign languages. It was hot and the thick air stank of sea water, coal smoke, and rotten produce. He was sorry he hadn't left his coat at the hotel, but he'd worn it to hide his .44.

He stepped under an awning to cool off and buy some fruit. The narrow shop was clean, considering, and the fruit and vegetables looked fresh and a cut better than some he'd passed. A young dark gal in a black dress was sprinkling the piled produce with a watering can as her husband or brother talked to two other men. The little gal looked bashful, so Longarm waited politely for the fruit seller to finish with his other customers. But Longarm couldn't help noticing it wasn't an ordinary transaction. The shopkeeper was a nice-looking young gent, dark and probably a Greek. The other two men looked American and mean. One growled something low at the Greek and he shouted, "No, no, and again no! I pay good money for my produce. I sell it at a modest profit. I can't afford to pay you what you ask, even if I thought I needed this protection business."

One of the bullies said, "You need it, George. We've been very easy on you up to now, you being new on the street. But how would it look if word got around that you didn't want to do business with us?"

His partner picked up a tomato, dropped it on the floor, and stepped on it. "Yeah. Folks would think they didn't need protection from—uh—accidents."

Young George stared down at his ruined tomato and gasped, "Hey, are you crazy?"

The bigger one pushed him. "No, *you* are," he said. "Nobody refuses to pay protection on this block!"

The girl dropped her watering can and started yelling at them in her own lingo to leave old George alone. So one of them pushed her, too, and said, "Shut up, you stupid bitch."

Longarm sighed and said, "That does it. Show's over, boys."

They both turned to stare tough at him. One said, "Get

lost, chump, unless you want a fat lip. We're having a private business meeting, see?"

"I noticed. And, like I said, it's over. But you'd best pay for that tomato before you leave."

They exchanged glances and grinned. Then they both went for Longarm at the same time. Somehow he'd been expecting they might, so he stepped out onto the walk for elbow room, and swung at the biggest one first.

He landed a right to the jaw. But the thug was only staggered and the other one was boring in with a set of brass knuckles he'd produced from somewhere. Fortunately, he led with his right. Longarm blocked it, threw a counterpunch, and made hash out of his face. So the bully lay down to sleep it off while Longarm braced for the other one's next move.

But there wasn't any. George had grabbed the one still on his feet by the shoulder and spun him around to smash him flat with his own fist. Old George didn't fight scientifically, but he was likely strong from heaving boxes all day, so he put his man on the pavement, too.

The commotion had attracted a crowd. Someone cried out, "Jeez, who put Dutch and Brassy on the walk?"

Another yelled back, "George the Greek and that tall guy. I gotta get my stuff inside and put up the grate! Them lunatics just declared war on the Dusters!"

Longarm grinned across the carnage at George. "You hit pretty good," he told the young man.

The Greek stared soberly back and said, "I am George Metaxis Callas. You have me forever in your debt. But you'd better leave. These creatures are like the bananas I sell. They are yellow, and they come in bunches."

"I don't see *you* running, George. My name's Custis Long, by the way."

"I won't forget it. The reason I do not run is that there is nowhere for me to run. But this is not your fight, Mr. Long."

"Sure it is. I started it, didn't I?"

The young Greek girl came over, took Longarm's hand, and stroked it.

Callas said, "This is my sister, Iris. She does not speak English, but you know what she wishes to say." He added something in Greek and the girl protested. He spoke more sharply and she sighed and went back inside.

Her brother turned to Longarm. "I told her to go upstairs and lock the door."

Longarm said, "Good move," as he nudged one of the fallen thugs with his boot tip. "Are you just fixing to lay there like a plank all day?" he asked the downed bully.

The man groaned. "This is going to cost you, cowboy."

Longarm kicked him in the ear. It put him back to sleep and made the whole crowd gasp with awe.

A pair of uniformed coppers shoved through just then to ask what was going on. Longarm kept still and let the Greek tell them. The coppers grinned at each other. "Wonders never cease on this beat," one said. "I don't suppose you'd be willing to press charges, of course?"

Someone in the crowd yelled, "Don't do it, George. It ain't smart."

The Greek looked at Longarm. Longarm said, "Do it. They're already mad at us. Even if the judge lets 'em off, they'll know *you're* mad, too. What have you got to lose?"

George nodded and told the coppers he'd be proud to press charges. So the coppers put the cuffs on the bullies, woke them up with the watering can Iris had left on the floor, and dragged them off as the crowd marveled. Someone said, "I can't believe it! I thought the Dusters had the coppers paid off!"

A heavy-set gray-haired man came out of the crowd to wrap his arms around George and sob at him in Greek. Then he pulled Longarm in and said, "I am so proud of my countryman. He is a credit to our nation and I, Skouras, am ashamed. I am crazy. I know I am crazy. But I, Skouras, will stand with you!"

A younger, husky man in a white apron came over and said, "Count me in, too. I ain't Greek, but I'm tired of

110

paying off the Dusters, too!" He turned and bellowed, "Hey, whaddayah say? Gino Rizzio's had enough. So if the Greeks stand, Italy stands!"

Three other tough-looking shopkeepers stepped in to join them. A mean-looking giant with red hair came over, shrugged, and said, "What the hell, count County Clare in. They're going to bust all our stands anyway, so let's make 'em work at it."

Someone in the crowd said, "Jeez, you've all been out in the sun too long!" but a short, wiry gent with black curly hair stepped out of the pack with a broom handle and growled, "Faith, a Kerry man's as tough as anyone from Clare!"

A big, bearded fruit peddler followed, looking sort of sheepish as he asked, "Can a Jew join this revolution?"

George was grinning now as he told Longarm, "We've got an outside chance. Let the Dusters come. We'll all be ready for them!"

There was a gleeful roar of approval and some more merchants stepped out of the crowd to stand and be counted.

Longarm held up a hand for silence. "Hold on, boys. I admire your guts, but you ain't good at tactics. Are you gents really ready to stand up for your rights?"

"By God, we'll stand and *fight!*" said the Kerry man.

Longarm shook his head. "Bad tactics. You're giving all the options to the enemy. By now, the friends of those two gents the coppers carried off will have heard all about it. They'll be making plans to pay us back. But there's no way to tell when and where they'll hit first, see?"

George said, "You're right. They can choose the time and direction of their attack. But what can we do about that?"

"Choose our *own* time and such, of course. Do you boys know the headquarters of the rascals?"

The red-headed man from County Clare said, "I do. Sure it's an old abandoned brewery over across the tracks. The Dusters meet there to plan their divilment."

Longarm nodded. "Well, since they seem to plan so

much of it, it seems to me that'd be a good place to find them. If you boys are serious, we'd best move in on them right now!"

The men looked mighty sober at the thought of marching on the enemy in his own lair. Then the Jewish gent said, "I like it. It makes sense."

The Clare man said, "Follow me, then," and they all did.

As the little army of angry merchants headed for the corner, a new arrival called out, "What's going on?"

One who'd hung back shouted, "They're going after the Dusters!"

The man who'd asked the question gave a war whoop. "It's about time! Count me in!"

By the time they reached Tenth Avenue, the posse had grown to a small army. George, striding beside Longarm with a barrel stave in hand, said, "I can't believe it! I thought I was the only one willing to stand up for my rights."

"You were, till you *done* it," Longarm said. "Most toughs depend on the fact that civilized folk don't fight in bunches, as a rule. No sensible man likes to take on a gang alone. But, given some leadership, the good can be just as ornery as the bad."

They were, that afternoon. The mob of Ninth Avenue merchants hit the old brewery screaming for blood. Someone in the gang had spotted them, so the door was barred on the inside, but they just busted through. They were strong old boys from all the honest work they done. The Hudson Dusters couldn't say as much.

They tried. They had to. But a man gets out of shape drinking beer and just beating up on folks smaller than he is. So the melee was almost unfairly one-sided. The Hudson Dusters were badly outnumbered and considerably rattled to be bearded in their own den. As Longarm and his pals busted in, one Hudson Duster produced a shotgun, but Longarm blew his face off with a .44 slug, and after that it got confusing. Longarm only got to hit a couple of Dusters. He was at the disadvantage of having to be careful

112

who he hit in the free-for-all. But the merchants the gang had been shaking down seemed to know them all personally, and they didn't like the Dusters much.

By the time the police arrived it was all over. Some of the Hudson Dusters had escaped by running off like rats, and most of the ones draped over the crates and beer pipes or just stretched out on the cement floor seemed likely to recover in time. The coppers didn't see fit to arrest anyone on Longarm's side once he flashed his badge and explained the situation to them. They started dragging the Hudson Dusters out and when one woke up and asked what was going on, the coppers told him he was under arrest for disturbing the peace and then knocked him out again.

As he stood outside watching how the coppers dealt with the riffraff, Detective Sergeant Mulligan and another plain-clothesman came over to him. Mulligan said, "I might have known I'd find you here, Longarm. You sure are a noisy guy, you know?"

"I've noticed New York is a tougher town than the folks in Dodge might think," Longarm replied. I moseyed up this way to see if the Teaneck Kid might be hanging out in Hell's Kitchen, but I failed to see his face in the crowd."

"You moseyed, huh? They tell me there's a Hudson Duster with a bullet in his head. How do you think we'd better write that up?"

Longarm looked sheepish. "Suicide?" he asked.

Mulligan tried not to laugh. "That sounds reasonable. Wojensky told us about that other 'suicide' over in Kip's Bay. So we owe you. But it sure was quieter on this beat before you showed up. Did you get an answer yet on whether we can work together or not?"

Longarm shook his head. "I'm still waiting to hear from my boss in Denver. But, as long as I got you in a friendly mood, are there any other interesting gangs like the Hudson Dusters here in Hell's Kitchen?"

Mulligan shrugged. "Not showing their faces. This vig-ilante business you've started figures to have the boyos off the street for a while. How did you turn all these fruit peddlers into tigers? We've hardly ever been able to get them to press charges."

"I teach by example. Since Hell's Kitchen looks a mite quiet right now, what's further north?"

"Forget it. The town thins out to the north and you wouldn't want to go to Harlem."

"What's in Harlem?"

"Nothing you'd be interested in. Harlem's a quiet, sort of high-toned residential neighborhood. There's hardly ever any crime up in Harlem and I don't want you bothering the folks up there."

"All right. I'll take your word Harlem's sort of sissy. Where else might I run into the rougher element?"

Mulligan shrugged. "I can't think of any place we haven't pretty well covered. Foreign neighborhoods like Little Italy and German Town don't sound right for the Teaneck Kid, and our street people say he's not running with any of the well-known English-speaking gangs."

"Well, he started his own gang out West. Maybe he means to start his own back here," Longarm said thoughtfully.

Mulligan shook his head and said, "It's not easy to start your own gang in New York, Longarm."

"Why not?" Longarm asked. "*I* just did all right, didn't I?"

# Chapter 8

Longarm studied on Mulligan's words as he walked alone back toward Paddy's Market. He could see that most of the New York gangs recruited from friends and relations in their own neighborhoods, and New York neighborhoods were tight. Out West, the Teaneck Kid had recruited drifters he'd met on the skid rows of trail towns. If he meant to do the same here, he'd have to recruit transients, not neighborhood toughs.

If he was still in New York at all. Nobody'd seen hide nor hair of the rascal for three days. He and the sidekick who'd helped him to escape from the Tombs might have caught the first train out. The police were watching the trains and ferries *now*, but, of course, they hadn't for the first seventy-two hours, when they'd thought the Kid was in Longarm's custody.

Longarm stopped on a corner to get his bearings. He

knew there wasn't much chance of cutting the trail on the crowded sidewalks of New York, even if the Teaneck Kid was still in town. It was tempting just to toss in a bad hand and get up from the table. But, on the other hand, it was the only game in town. He had a pretty gal to meet that evening and another pretty gal was holding a horse for him. He decided he'd stick around till he spotted some sign or till Billy Vail told him to come on home. The question, now, was which way he headed next. The infernal Teaneck Kid could be any direction from here.

He'd just decided to walk over to Broadway and follow it downtown when a rat-faced gent sidled up to him and said, "Come with me. Madame Alice wants a word with you."

Longarm looked him over. "Who might Madame Alice be?" he asked.

The oily man said, "She'd better tell you herself. She sent me to get you. Are you coming or not?"

Longarm looked at his watch and saw he had some time left to kill. "May as well," he said, "but it's only fair to warn you that if Madame Alice is a real madam, I never pay for such services."

The rat-faced man led Longarm up the avenue to a brown-stone house. The lamp over the door wasn't lit in broad daylight, but Longarm could see that it had red glass. The pimp, or whatever he was, led Longarm up the steps and ushered him inside. The vestibule was dark. Through an open archway Longarm saw some gals lounging about on red plush sofas in their underwear.

The oily gent turned Longarm over to a colored maid in a trim uniform. She led him upstairs and into the madam's room.

The windows were covered with red velvet, and so was Madame Alice. She sat under a lit ceiling lamp. He was surprised to see that she was young and pretty. Her hair was red, her gown low-cut. She wore more paint than a cigar-store Indian, but she had aristocratic bone structure and could have passed as a high-toned lady if she'd wanted to.

As the maid left them alone, Madame Alice said, "So you're the big bastard who kicked the living shit out of the Dusters, huh? What's your name, cowboy?"

"I'm Custis Long, and I had a little help with the Hudson Dusters, Madame Alice. What's this all about?"

"I owe you," she said. "Everyone in Hell's Kitchen owes you. They'll be back in business in a month or so, but meanwhile I'll only have to pay off the precinct captain. The Dusters were shaking me down for a couple of hundred a week. How much would you cost me to see that it never happens again?"

"I fear I ain't likely to be in town by the time they're back in business, ma'am," he said. "But now that I've proved they ain't so tough, you ought to be able to hire some muscle to protect you from the rascals."

"Not as big as yours, damn it. But I ought to show a better profit for a time, thanks to you. So, like I said, I owe you."

She heisted her skirt, exposing a length of nicely-turned leg as she took a wad of bills from under her red lace garter and started peeling some money off.

Longarm said, "Hold on. I don't take money from ladies."

She looked surprised. "How the hell am I to pay you off, then? I don't serve customers myself, but sit down and I'll have my girls trot through for inspection. You can pick any one you like. Hell, pick *two*, if you feel frisky this afternoon."

Longarm sat down on a nearby red velvet sofa. "I don't consider myself a customer—no offense—so I'll pass on the *hired help,* ma'am."

Madame Alice looked him over thoughtfully and murmured, "Well, I'm a bit out of practice, for I don't have many friends, and the madam isn't supposed to screw anyone else. But, what the hell, you're a good-looking man, so if you think I'm good-looking, too..."

As she started peeling Longarm said, "Hold on, Madame Alice. Let's just talk for a minute. I consider you a right handsome woman, too, but I got me a gal. What I'm really looking for is conversation with a woman of the world like you. You might say I'm a seeker of knowledge. I ain't all that horny."

Madame Alice frowned, sighed, and said, "All right. What do you want to know? How a nice girl like me got into this awful business?"

"I may as well confess, I tote a badge," Longarm said. "But don't let it fret you. I'm Federal and there's nothing in the U.S. Constitution about your notions of free enterprise."

She blinked, laughed uncertainly, and said, "I might have known. But I still owe you, so all right. Who are you looking for in Hell's Kitchen? You just kicked the shit out of the Hudson Dusters."

"That was just a side show, Madame Alice. If New York works like Dodge and Denver, all the gals in your line of work keep in touch about new faces in town, right?"

She nodded and said, "There's an awful lot of faces in the Tenderloin, but we do pass the word on stiffs, sadists, or rats wandering about with a dose. We're in competition, but one hand washes the other, if you know what I mean."

"I do. Sporting ladies usually notice gents who've just come into sudden wealth and act sort of nervous about sudden noises, too, right?"

"Sure. It's a real bother to be raided by the coppers. We'd rather tip the law off ahead of time and build some character with the police. Like I said, one hand washes the other."

Longarm nodded. "Well, let's wash some hands, then." He told her about the Teaneck Kid, describing his appearance and the way he liked to play Wild West badman.

Madame Alice shook her head. "Nobody like that's been here. But I'll run it down the grapevine. Where will I find you if this would-be Jesse James is hiding out somewhere with a businesswoman?"

He told her about his hotel and warned her to be discreet, as he was sort of engaged to a proper gal.

Madame Alice sniffed. "Shacked up with an amateur, eh? Don't worry, I'll send a man with a note. Is this tootsie-wootsie any good in bed?"

"Tolerable, ma'am. I hardly ever go to bed with anyone who's *awful,* if I can help it."

She frowned and said, "I'll bet I'm better." So he took out his watch. He still had over an hour before getting downtown became a desperate matter. He was curious about Madame Alice's build, too. But it seemed ridiculous to dally with a whore, when the real thing would be waiting for him in just a little while.

Madame Alice stood up and proceeded to shuck her red dress casually, like they were old friends. He wanted to keep her friendly, as a possible informant. He didn't see how he could if he acted like a sissy, or, worse, a man who didn't admire her fine figure.

Admiring her figure wasn't all that hard. Madame Alice emerged from her red velvet built firm and hourglass. He saw that he'd been right about her hair being dyed. In truth she was a natural blonde. She draped her duds over the back of a chair and stood brazenly before him, unpinning her long hair with her arms and pretty tits upraised, and Long-arm started to feel upraised, too. So he took off his own duds and they got right to it.

They did it on the voluptuous red sofa. He knew whores doing it for pleasure found it novel to be treated like old-fashioned gals, so he just mounted her old-fashioned, and, sure enough, she liked it.

She smiled up at him as she wrapped her legs around his waist and said, "Heavens, there's even more to you than meets the eye! Do you like my pussy?"

He started moving in her as he replied, "I like everything about you, Madame Alice. Would it upset you if I kissed you?"

"On the lips? Well, it's an unusual request, but we aim to please."

So he started swapping spit with her as she aided and abetted his activities at her other end with considerable bumping and grinding. He knew most men didn't kiss gals like Madame Alice. That Casanova cuss had been right to suggest treating ladies like whores and whores like ladies. Nobody did it better than a businesswoman taking time off the job with a friend. Men were just the opposite; they screwed better when they felt a mite detached. So everybody on the red sofa enjoyed what they were doing, and when they came up for air, Madame Alice marveled, "I can't believe it. I really came. Could you—ah—stick around for a while?"

He said that he could, of course. Billie didn't know he'd been late for their noon meeting, so she ought not to get too sore if he showed up for supper a mite late. She had her own key and she might like to bathe and freshen up whilst she waited for him. He hoped she'd want to go right to supper when he got there. Madame Alice was moving her hips again and he knew he'd leave here drained of inspiration for a spell.

Longarm knew he was going to be late for supper when he said goodbye to Madame Alice. She said to come back any time and promised to send him word if any whore in town mentioned any cowboys hiding out in the Tenderloin.

He caught a street car downtown, and as it crept and clanged through the evening rush hour he saw he was going to be even later than he'd figured. He hoped his girl reporter would be a good sport about it. He hoped she wouldn't want to kiss and make up in bed, either. He needed a hot meal and a few hours' recuperation before he could be a man again. Tearing off a quick one in an alley with Dreadful Doris was one thing. But he'd just had probably a hundred dollars' worth of professional bare-ass bedroom acrobatics free. Madame Alice sure had suggested some odd positions once they'd busted the ice back there.

Longarm got off on Canal Street and started legging it for his hotel. As he reached his block, he saw a horse-drawn fire engine and a police ambulance up ahead. A big crowd stood about the entrance of the Majestic, so Longarm walked faster. As he joined the crowd and started elbowing his way through, Detective Wojensky hailed him.

"They told us you were staying here," he said. "You sure lead an exciting life!"

"I've been uptown in Hell's Kitchen. So, whatever it is, I didn't do it. What's going on?"

The ambulance started pulling away. Wojensky pointed after it with his chin and said, "It was a bomb. It got that lady reporter from the *Sun*."

Longarm gasped in horror. "My God—was she hurt bad?"

Wojensky shrugged. "As bad as it gets. She's on her way to the morgue. They sent me over because I knew you both. They tell us inside that she was sharing a room with you."

"Let's not put *that* in any fool report! I always hire a double room, in case I meet a lady. Miss McArtle was meeting me here for an interview."

"Yeah. It's the least we can do for her. As we put it together, she got here ahead of you and went up to your room to wait. The bomb was placed inside with a trip wire attached to the doorknob. She opened the door and—She wasn't messed up too bad by the blast. The sons of bitches used a small charge of dynamite with a lot of nails and other scrap. She never knew what hit her. One ten-penny nail went right through her skull."

Longarm walked over to a lamppost, balled up his fist, and hit it. It split two knuckles and didn't make him feel a bit better. Wojensky joined him, saying, "Take it easy. You know, of course, who that bomb was meant for?"

Longarm nodded bleakly and said, "It would have got me, if I hadn't been late getting back. The gent who said virtue was its own reward was full of shit. I think I know who done it," he went on. "A man pretending to be a lawman was going from hotel to hotel, asking if I was registered there. He describes the same as the rascal who pretended to be at the Tombs. A hotel clerk down the street said he even wore a Stetson."

121

Wojensky whistled softly. "That fits. It adds up to the Teaneck Kid still being in town, too. They were crazy to go after you, Longarm. I was just about to throw in the sponge on the case."

Longarm nodded. "That makes two of us. So let's study on what it means. Betwixt us, we've pretty well covered the places you'd expect to find a desperado on the dodge."

"I'm way ahead of you. The two of them are hiding out someplace good—so good they don't want to leave town. Only you and the turnkeys at the Tombs know the Teaneck Kid by sight. None of us knows the confederate. The only reason they could have for killing you is...what? That's where I get stuck."

"Move over and let me stand in the mud, too," Longarm said. "If they're staying in some decent neighborhood boarding house, hotel, or private residence, their best play would have been just to lay low till I gave up and went back out West."

"Maybe they don't expect you to give up?"

"Hell, everybody gives up, sooner or later, if they don't find anything. If they knew enough about me to impersonate me they had to know my office never transferred me back East permanent. No, they had a reason. The Teaneck Kid has to show his face somewhere in town where I might see it. He might have a job or something calling for him to be someplace public. Someplace he's afraid I'd trip over him if I just keep wandering all over New York City."

"There's a lot of city to wander, Longarm. What about the guards who'd know him from his stay in the Tombs? Do you think they're in danger?"

Longarm thought, shook his head, and said, "He's had three days to go after them, and he didn't. But that's an interesting notion. Where would I be likely to wind up that a New York copper wouldn't?"

"There's no such place," said Wojensky flatly. "At least a dozen men from the Tombs would recognize the kid *and* his confederate on sight. They live all over town. Uniform blues pull special duty sometimes, too. There's no way the

Teaneck Kid and his pal could be sure a copper who knew them wouldn't turn up posted almost anywhere in public."

Longarm said, "Maybe the Kid's just mad at me. Let's go inside and see if anyone left any other messages for me."

Wojensky followed Longarm into the lobby. The badly shaken desk clerk handed him a telegram and said, "We're going to have to ask you to stay somewhere else, Mr. Long. We try to run a respectable hotel here, and..."

"Shut up," Longarm cut in. "I'm staying here for respectable reasons. I'm the law and I'm expecting more messages. I'm also hopeful that the son of a bitch who just tried to kill me might come back so's I can get a look at him."

The clerk said, "Oh my God!"

Longarm opened the wire from his home office and read it. Marshal Billy Vail said he wanted both the crooks on Federal charges. Longarm didn't mention that to Wojensky. Vail went on to say that, while he'd told the marshal's office in Kansas he'd be sending a man to transport the prisoner, he hadn't said who and he hadn't described Longarm to them. He hadn't told the New York police what Longarm looked like, either. So that eliminated a lot of peace officers. But if Vail hadn't told anyone who was coming, how in thunder could the crooks have known it would be him?

He snapped his fingers and headed back out to the street. Wojensky followed, asking where they were going. "There's a Western Union office down on the corner," Longarm said. "The confederate works as a bounty hunter and compares notes with other rascals in the business. I had a set-to with a so-called private detective on the train here. He knew who I was and where I was headed, for a lady told me he went through my bag and read my papers whilst I was out of my seat. He got off to send a night letter shortly thereafter. I thought he was sending it to Chicago, but now I think he wired the interesting news to someone here in New York. It's my hope the Omaha law can tell us more about it. I left Mr. Frog in their care."

"Mr. Frog?"

"His name's Marcy, he says, but he looks like a frog. His name figures to be Mud if he refuses to tell us who he sent that night letter to!"

They entered the telegraph office and Longarm got off a message to Omaha. The Western Union agent said they ought to have a reply in less than an hour since, like most modern outfits, the Omaha law was patched into the cross-country wires direct. Longarm and Wojensky went next door for a smoke and a beer as Longarm filled the New Yorker in on the details of his adventure with Mr. Frog—leaving out the most interesting parts about the princess, of course.

Wojensky said, "We may be getting somewhere if that bastard in the Omaha jail contacted a New York detective agency. It narrows the suspects down to a reasonable mob."

But Longarm shook his head. "Mr. Frog didn't seem to have a license. That's why he's in the Omaha jail. Many a hired bully boy just *says* he's licensed. The rascal at the Tombs said he was a Federal deputy, and we know *that* was a fib. Lots of lawyers, business firms, and such hire guns or strongarms without going through any formalities. Old Mr. Frog was chasing folk for a bail bondsman. Let's study on that. The Teaneck Kid was in your Tombs. Am I correct in guessing runners for bail bondsmen visit the holding tanks fairly regular?"

"Sure. That's how they do business. But the prisoner we were holding for you was being held without bail on a Federal murder charge. He might have talked to many a bondsman, but even if they'd wanted to, they couldn't bail him out."

"No. On the other hand, he might have convinced someone in that line of work he surely wanted out. The jailhouse gang ain't as decent even as whores, but, like whores, they keep each other posted and their job is to get crooks out of jail, right?"

Wojensky whistled, took out his notebook, and made a notation. "I'll check that angle out. But bail bondsmen *do* have licenses to worry about. So, scum or not, they don't spring anyone for free. The Teaneck Kid didn't have any money on him when he was picked up. He'd just escaped from Leavenworth, right?"

"Wrong. Everyone forgets he made it back East and wandered about at large for a spell before he got picked up on another killing charge. There ain't no way to say what he might or might not have stolen before he had that last shootout. What can you tell me about the shootout?"

Wojensky hesitated. "I'm not supposed to work with you. But I owe you. So, what the hell. It was a simple enough case. He was walking down Forty-seventh Street with a married woman who apparently made a habit of picking up men, when her husband accosted them. There was an argument, the husband took a swing, and the Teaneck Kid pulled his gun and blew him away. It was early evening in a respectable neighborhood, so a brace of coppers over on the avenue responded to the shots and he ran right into their arms. He put up a little fight, but then he just gave up, confessed he was the notorious Teaneck Kid—and you know the rest."

"No, I don't. Tell me more about the love of his life. I'd like a word with her."

"You can't have it. Her sudden widowhood inspired her to go home to Kentucky. That's where she and her late husband came from. They were only in town for the racing season. She enjoyed other sports, too. They say she'd once been caught in bed with a jockey. Fortunately, not by her husband."

"Old Teaneck's sort of horsey, too," Longarm said. "The widow sounds rich. If she was fond of him . . ."

"Forget it. She was fond of her husband, too, despite the way she carried on. She went home to the children they had in Kentucky. I can't see her helping her husband's killer escape."

Longarm couldn't, either. He swallowed some beer and said, "Speaking of gals and horses, I left a cow pony with

125

a lady I met up in the park a spell back. Her name's Monica Van Tassel. Can you tell me if she's part of the New York sporting set?"

Wojensky blinked. "You met the Widow Van Tassel? And she *spoke* to you?"

"She had to. I was holding her horse. What do you know about her?"

"She's from one of the old patroon families. She wouldn't associate with the likes of that Kentucky racehorse owner's woman. Patroons hardly speak to anyone."

"I'll bite. What's a patroon?"

"Old New York Dutch society. They're such snobs they don't even allow their children to play with the Astors or the Vanderbilts. The Vanderbilts are New York Dutch, too, but they've only had their money a little while. You say Monica Van Tassel's keeping a cow pony for you?"

"Yep. She acted neighborly enough to me. Spoke polite to a colored groom, too. I didn't take her for a snob."

Wojensky smiled bitterly and said, "That's the mark of a true snob. That groom probably makes more money than you and me put together. People like the Van Tassels never throw their weight around. They don't have to. When you've got that kind of money—and the power that goes with it—you don't yell at people who annoy you; you just step on them, like ants. I'd steer clear of Monica Van Tassel if I were you."

"Well, sooner or later I have to take that cow pony out of her stable. I'll watch where I spit. How long has she been a widow, and how come?"

"Hell, I don't know the details. You'd be surprised how seldom I get invited to weddings and funerals up in that part of town. Her husband was Jaçob Van Tassel, a land baron up the river. He wasn't a bad man, for one of them. Got run over by a street car down near Wall Street, maybe three or four years ago. And before you ask, his widow ain't the merry kind. She enjoys a good reputation even in the stuffy society. She does a lot of charity work. She can afford it."

126

Longarm pursed his lips. "I noticed a charity mission over on the Bowery last night."

Wojensky said, "Forget it. Mrs. Van Tassel's *charitable* with her money, not *foolish* with it. She funds an orphanage in the Blooming Dale and runs a night school to teach immigrants how to read and write in English. Her *servants* would be too stuck up to talk to the Teaneck Kid's crowd."

"She sounds like a nice lady. How come you're so down on her?"

"You'd have to grow up in New York to understand how the rest of us feel about people like her. It's bad enough that they *act* like their shit don't stink. The hell of it is, it *don't!* The new rich get falling-down drunk, get their servant girls in trouble, and create all sorts of juicy scandals for the newspapers to print. But the old patroons just keep to themselves, never doing anything improper, as they waft sedately through life, getting ever richer."

Longarm drained his stein and suggested they go back to Western Union. A return wire from Omaha was waiting for them. Longarm read it, balled it up with a curse, and said, "Mr. Frog is at large, too! The infernal Omaha judge let him off with a fine—and now nobody knows where *he* is either!"

# Chapter 9

It was after sunset when Longarm marched up the steps of the Van Tassel mansion on Fifth Avenue and used the big brass knocker. A butler who looked proud enough to be a Mexican general opened the door and stared at him like a wooden Indian. Longarm told him who he was and why he'd come.

The butler said, "Oh, yes, Deputy Long. Madame instructed me you might be coming to call. Walk right this way, sir."

Longarm followed the rascal across a wide expanse of checkerboard marble and into a drawing room big enough to use for a railroad station waiting room. The room was tastefully furnished, save for a mighty odd-looking lamp on a table near a big tan sofa by the cold marble fireplace. The butler took Longarm's hat, waved him to a seat, and said he'd tell Madame he was here.

A little while later, the willowy ash blonde Monica Van Tassel came in, wearing yet another tan outfit. This one seemed less suited for riding in the park. Longarm didn't know all that much about women's duds, but he could see the simply cut summer dress cost more than the one Madame Alice had started out with across town. As he got to his feet she smiled and said, "Please don't rise on my account," as she held out her hand.

He didn't know what she expected him to do with her fool hand, so he shook it. She raised an eyebrow but didn't say anything as she sat down beside him, picked up a little bell, and tinkled it without saying why. She said, "Your dear little mare has been reshod. I hope you don't mind, but the grooms reported that her horseshoes were badly nailed."

Longarm wondered when was the last time he'd cleaned his own nails as he smiled sheepishly and replied, "That was very kind of you, ma'am. I only borrowed the mare. But if your hands said she needed reshoeing, I'll take their word for it. How much do I owe you?"

She told him not to be silly. He could see how this kind of Madame could spook folks worse than Madame Alice's kind. It seemed hard to believe old Monica ate and drank like ordinary folks. She was in charge of this house and everybody in it and it showed.

A maid came in with a tea set on a silver tray and set it on a rosewood table in front of them like she was delivering a gift to the manger. Monica thanked her sweetly, like a regular human gal. Longarm knew that was the mark of a woman who'd bossed servants since she was old enough to talk. She felt no need to bluster or keep them in their place. No servant had ever sassed her back in her entire life.

As she poured the tea, Longarm studied her profile. It belonged on a cameo. Every hair was in place. There wasn't a blemish on her healthy tan. Blemishes knew better than to mess with a Van Tassel, and while gals who weren't as sure of themselves tried to keep from getting suntanned as they prissed about in the sunlight under parasols, old Monica knew nobody would dare to tell *her* she was unfashionable. That was likely why she didn't wear widow's weeds, like any other gal might have. Everyone who knew her knew she was a widow, and she didn't care what anyone else might think. She wasn't wearing a wedding band or any other jewelry. There wasn't a trace of powder or paint on her, and her faint perfume smelled fresh, like wild flowers and green grass somewhere just upwind. He wondered what kind of underwear she wore, and told himself not to wonder. Her dress was just tight enough to show, without bragging, that she had to look beautiful all over. But she was as comfortable with her beauty as she was with her wealth. He didn't care what Wojensky said; he liked her.

She handed him his cup, saying, "I don't take sugar or cream. I forgot to ask if you did. Please forgive me. You see, I don't entertain much any more and—well—I'm still a bit upset about this afternoon."

"I like this tea just the way it is, ma'am. How come you're upset? That runaway wasn't all that much, if you ask me."

She frowned. "Runaway? Oh, you mean our meeting in the park across the way. That wasn't what upset me. It happened after you'd left. My silly Aunt Matilda came to call with my awful Cousin Freddy. I've never been able to stand either of them."

"Happens in the best of families. What did they do, spill tea on your carpet? That's a mighty handsome carpet, by the way."

"Thank you. It's a Persian. It was a more personal family matter. I really shouldn't talk about it."

He said, "Don't talk about it, then."

She laughed. "You're rather a strange person. I don't know why, but I *do* feel comfortable talking to you, and I have to tell somebody. It would never do for my friends or even the servants to know that my relatives have asked me for money again."

He nodded. "Lots of folks have kin like that, even when

131

they ain't rich. You felt bad about telling them no, huh?"

"Heavens, I couldn't *refuse* them! Poor Aunt Matilda has nobody else to turn to. She's made an awful mess of her inheritance." Her voice dropped to a whisper as she added, "They've been living on their capital!" It was as if she'd confided a family secret worse than incest.

Longarm knew just enough about money to understand she meant the aunt had managed to get herself in a fix by spending money faster than it came in.

Monica went on, "If only that useless Freddy would *do* something. But when I suggested he let me see about a seat on the Exchange for him, he looked as if he would burst out in tears."

"Some young gents are like that. How old's this useless cousin, ma'am?"

"He's almost thirty, and he's never worked a day in his life. He's not even interested in sports, for heaven's sake. I've never known anyone so—so *inert* as poor little Freddy Hoover. He was an awful sissy when we were little, as I recall. He was away from home for a while and we all hoped he was going to make something of himself out West, but he came back like the bad penny he is. I don't know why he just mopes about Aunt Matilda's house like a wraith instead of going out and getting some sort of position that would bring in a little money."

Longarm put his cup down. "Why go to work when you got rich relations you can sponge off?"

She sighed and said, "I'm afraid you're right. I really must learn to be more firm. But he seemed so upset this afternoon that I just didn't have the heart. He's always been a silly twit, but he was simply impossible today."

"He don't sound like much," Longarm said. "About that horse out back, ma'am. I've studied on what's to be done with her. I borrowed her over at the Kip's Bay Cow Town. So if I take her back, they'll likely find a new owner for her."

"Oh? What happened to her original owner?"

"He died. I'd best study on taking her off your hands."

But, as he started to ease his weight off the couch she asked, "Must you leave so early? I'm expecting another caller and—well—you'd be doing me a favor if you stayed until he left."

"Do tell. Who is this rascal you don't want to see alone, ma'am?"

"My broker, Peter Dekker. That is, he's supposed to be my broker, but he's been acting rather—ah—forward of late."

"I can see how that could be a problem for a pretty widow woman, ma'am. I reckon I can set a spell."

She shot him a curious look, started to say something, and turned to point at the nearby funny lamp he'd noticed, asking, "Do you think this suits the rest of the decor in here? I bought it on impulse, I'm afraid."

"I figured you might have. What's it supposed to be, a lamp, or some sort of sea monster?"

She said, "It's the new Art Nouveau style. It's all the rage in Paris this season."

"Well, it sure looks different, ma'am. If you like it, keep it. It's your house, ain't it?"

She laughed. "You do have a direct way of putting things. I wish I did. But, all right—who told you I was a widow? Have you been gossiping about me in the neighborhood?"

"I don't gossip much. I was told about you by the police. I told you I was a Federal deputy when we first met up."

"I'd forgotten. But why on earth would you ask the police about *me?*"

"It was volunteered when I told a detective I was coming up here this evening."

Naturally, she was interested, and naturally, he brought her up to date on his manhunt, leaving the dirty parts out.

She said, "My, you lead an interesting life. I've only heard of places like the Bowery and Hell's Kitchen. I've never been to them. Are the slums of New York really as bad as they say?"

"Worse. I had this town down sort of sissy, too."

Before they could get into it, the butler ushered in a tall, sardonic, smooth-shaven cuss dressed up like the late Prince Albert of England. He didn't looked pleased to find Longarm there. That was all right; Longarm didn't like him, either. Peter Dekker looked like he thought his shit didn't stink, but Longarm was sure it did.

He said he'd come to jaw with Monica about stocks and bonds. He sat there droning on about percentage points and such while Monica nodded politely and Longarm tried to stay awake. He'd never heard a more tiresome conversation. But then his ears perked up as old Pete mentioned something he did know about.

Longarm said, "Hold on. I'd stay out of silver futures if I was you, folks. Silver ain't a good buy this year."

Peter Dekker smiled sort of nasty and asked, "Oh? I didn't get the impression you were too familiar with the market, Mr. Long."

"I ain't. I suspicion you'd look dumb trying to mill a stampede, too. The reason I know something about silver is that I was involved in some silver futures skullduggery out in Colorado a spell back. The price of silver is jumping up and down like a grasshopper with the itch. I've talked to experts, and they just don't know if it's likely to go up or down. So I'd bet on something safer, like dice, before I'd gamble on silver futures."

The broker looked at their hostess and asked, "Monica?"

"I don't want to buy silver futures on margin, Peter," she said. "I don't care if the market's going up or down. My late husband, and my late father as well, warned me never to buy anything on margin."

Dekker said, "A lot of people do, you know."

That turned out to be a dumb move. Monica's nostrils flared as she said, "Yes, my poor Aunt Matilda did a few years ago. This afternoon we had quite a discussion about her finances. I've been meaning to talk to you about a position for her son Freddy, Peter."

Dekker grimaced. "I wish you wouldn't. I've told you before, it's simply impossible to get him a position with our firm. The boy's just impossibly stupid and lazy, even if he is your cousin."

Monica started giving the young broker hell about her poor little Cousin Freddy, and after he'd taken it for a spell he looked at his watch and said he had another appointment, so she let him go.

As soon as they were alone together again, she burst out laughing. Longarm grinned, too, but said, "That was mighty cruel, ma'am."

"Yes, wasn't it?" she said. "I wonder if he thought we were lovers."

Longarm said, "I'd surely be game, but it would play hell with your reputation, wouldn't it?"

She laughed again. Then she sobered and added quickly, "Oh, I never meant to be unkind about our, well, social positions."

He smiled. "Sure you did. But I helped you shed that other gent because you were nice to my horse. I'd best get on down the road, now, ma'am."

She rose as he did, to lead him out the back way personally. The house went on forever, but they finally got out back and Monica told the groom to saddle up the cutting horse. As they waited, she looked up at Longarm thoughtfully and said, "I just had a rather silly idea."

"What are you aiming to do—buy another lamp?"

"No. I have to attend a social function tomorrow afternoon. Peter will be there, and of course he'll want to escort me home."

"So?"

"If I had an escort, he couldn't."

"That's true enough, ma'am. Why don't you ask one of the gents you know to take you there and back?"

"I'm afraid that could be jumping from the frying pan into the fire. I don't want to get involved with any of the eligibles in our crowd. I was wondering if *you'd* like to be my escort, Custis."

He snorted in disbelief. "You're right, it's silly. I'd ad-

135

mire taking you for a ride in the park or such, but we'd both look dumb if I was to escort you to a fancy shindig."

"The invitations don't call for formal attire, and it's just up the avenue a few blocks. It's a private luncheon and apt to be a dreadful bore, but I have to go. Please say you'll come along."

He shook his head. "Not hardly. Even if I wanted to look like a bull in a china shop, I figure to be busy tomorrow. I got to run over to Teaneck, New Jersey, and check it out. It's likely a wild-goose chase, but I don't know where else to look for the Teaneck Kid."

She said, "Ten Eck."

He said, "That's what I just said."

But Monica insisted, "You said Teaneck. That's not the way the name's pronounced. I know those awful people in New Jersey say Teaneck. They even spell it that way. But the town was named after the patroon family that founded it. The family name was, and is, Ten Eck."

The groom had his mount ready and it didn't seem to matter how some long-dead Dutchman had said "Teaneck." Then he thought harder, frowned down at her, and asked, "Did you say *is?* Are some of these Ten Eck folks still around New York ma'am?"

"Of course. It's a large patroon family as well as a very old one. Why do you ask?"

He said, "I ain't sure. If I took you to that fancy party up the avenue, would I be likely to meet up with some of these here Ten Ecks?"

"Of course. All the right people will be there. Do you really want to escort me to the gathering?"

"No, but I sure want to see some of them Ten Ecks, so I'd better. What time is this here shindig?"

She said he'd best pick her up around high noon or earlier, since they'd start serving about one. He said he'd be there with bells on. "I'd much rather you managed a decent tie," Monica said. "What did I say to make you change your mind? I'll have to remember it."

He grinned. "To tell you the truth, I wanted to see you

136

again, and you gave me an excuse, even if I look dumb. There's only one chance in a million one of them fancy Ten Ecks would tell me about a black sheep in the family, even if they have one. But it's worth a try."

"Heavens! You suspect the man you're after could be a Ten Eck?"

"Well, I doubt his name's Tweed, and he don't seem to hail from Teaneck, New Jersey, even though I was aiming to double check there. He had to get the fool name somewhere. It's the sort of trick a gent with a nasty sense of humor might see fit to play on a fancier friend or relation. So, like I said, I'll be here with bells on. I might even pick up a new tie."

# Chapter 10

Longarm had run out of obvious places to look for an owl-hoot in the big city. So he tried some sightseeing in the parts of Lower Manhattan he hadn't covered. Below Canal Street the island ran to a point like a wedge of cake. Longarm didn't move his long legs half as fast as most New Yorkers, but he covered ground as good. He was edgy from frustration—both kinds. It was starting to look like he'd never find the Teaneck Kid, and there'd be nobody waiting for him, now, in the new room the hotel had given him on the third floor.

The evening papers had said Billie McArtle's funeral would be held over in Brooklyn. Longarm wasn't planning on attending. He didn't know any of her kin, and he didn't want folks asking dumb questions. The police report had been decent to the poor gal, saying she'd been killed covering a story.

New York City's Chinatown was much smaller than the one in Frisco and the Teaneck Kid wasn't there. Longarm walked along Park Row, where all the newspapers were published, then cut over to City Hall Park. Despite the hour the little park was crowded with folks and pigeons. A man standing on a barrel was preaching that the Jews were trying to take over the world. Longarm didn't stop to listen. He already had it from another soap-box orator that it was the Freemasons. Out West they said it was the Mormons or the Chinese.

He circled the area, having a look-see at the gents on the benches and the grass. Some were playing checkers, some sleeping. A couple was billing and cooing on a bench under a knocked-out street lamp. Neither of the men looked like the Teaneck Kid.

He had a gander at the big fancy courthouse the late Boss Tweed had built for the city of New York. It was mighty fancy and must have cost a lot of money, but old Boss Tweed had said it cost ten times as much, then put the difference in his pocket. That was one of the reasons he'd ended his career on Blackwell's Island. It was likely the reason the Teaneck Kid admired him so. Out West the Kid had gone out of his way to seem like a big bad man. The ornery young dude had started out like a boy playing cowboys and Indians and then just naturally drifted into really killing folks.

Longarm ambled down to Wall Street to see what all the fuss was about. Wall Street was shorter and more dull than he'd expected. It started at a graveyard and ran down to the river. The banks and brokerage houses on either side were shut down for the night, of course. He saw lights and activity in the distance, but when he headed that way and turned a corner he found himself in an all-night fish market.

There was another big all-night market over on the Hudson side. That one sold farm produce carted or floated in from all around. It surely took a lot of food to keep a town this size going. There was a neighborhood of Arab folks living near the Washington Market. Longarm didn't talk Arab, so he couldn't ask how they'd gotten there.

He found the gaslit entrance to Delmonico's, but didn't go into the big eatery to look for anybody. He'd already eaten in a saloon near his hotel and the folks going in and out of Delmonico's looked a mite fancy for the likes of him and the riffraff he was looking for. His theory was that the Teaneck Kid might be the black sheep of a respectable New York family, but he ran with lowlifes now, and he'd hardly dare show his face in such a public place no matter how he was dressed. Longarm wasn't the only lawman looking for the son of a bitch.

It only took a few minutes for Longarm to explore the Battery Park, where the cake wedge came to a point as the two rivers joined to flow on out through the Narrows to the wide Atlantic. The harbor lights looked pretty on the water, but Longarm had seen boats before, so he headed back to his hotel.

He got there before midnight, picked up some messages at the desk, and went upstairs with the reading material he'd picked up.

The killers came much later, around four o'clock.

Even Canal Street, out front, had quieted by four in the morning, though it was still brightly lit. The killers moved up the alley behind the hotel and eased up the newfangled wrought-iron fire stairs in the back of the Majestic. The hallway outside Longarm's room was dimly lit by a single gas jet. As the killers climbed in the low-silled window down at the end of the hall, one of them shut off the gas valve of the nightlight.

They moved in almost complete darkness to Longarm's door and listened. There was no light coming from under the door.

One of them took a skeleton key out and whispered, "Don't light that thing till I tell you."

The other man, who had a bomb in his hands, snorted

141

and replied, "Tell me how to open a bottle of beer, why don't you? Are you sure this is his room and that the bastard's in there?"

"Now who's telling someone how to open a bottle of beer? This is the room they moved him to. He went to bed alone, so he has to be asleep. I got the latch. Light the fuse."

The one with the bomb struck a match on the doorjamb. Longarm didn't want him to set off another bomb in the Majestic, so he popped out of the broom closet he'd been staked out in and snapped, "Freeze!"

The heavy-set one closer to Longarm whirled, gun in hand. That was poor thinking, since Longarm never told anyone to freeze when he didn't have the drop on him. Longarm's double-action .44 coughed twice in the darkness. He crabbed sideways to get away from his own muzzle flashes as some fool opened a door down the hall just as the man with the bomb ran past.

Longarm yelled, "Shut that goddamn door!"

The other hotel guest vanished.

Longarm had one on the floor, but by now the one with the bomb had made it to the hall window and out onto the fire stairs. He'd lit his fuse and was winding up to throw the bomb.

Longarm put a bullet in his chest and the bomber went over the rail, still holding his bomb. It went off on the way down to the alley pavement and shattered a lot of glass windows.

Longarm knew that one wasn't going anywhere, so he relit the hall lamp and had a closer look at the one he'd downed near his empty room's door. He rolled the rascal over with his boot and blinked in surprise.

"Howdy, Mr. Frog," he muttered. "You should have quit whilst you was ahead. I'd figured you must have wired your pals here in New York that I was coming. I'm surprised you was dumb enough to come here to join the party. You had time enough to catch up and pass me, thanks to my layover in Chicago. But you know all that, Marcy. Let's talk about

142

who you're working with here in New York City."

The wounded fat man couldn't have said much even if he'd wanted to. One of Longarm's rounds had hulled his vest, the other had hit him in his fat throat. He lay there glaring hate and fear, gargling on his own blood. By the time the desk downstairs sent two uniformed coppers up to join them Mr. Frog was dead.

Longarm had wisely pinned his badge on his lapel and holstered his reloaded gun, so the coppers knew right off he was on their side. Longarm left one of them to mind the corpse and led the other one down the fire stairs to see how much was left of the other rascal.

From the waist down, the corpse in the alley was a tall gent in yellow shoes and green pants. From the waist up he was only rags, bones, and hash.

The copper whistled and said, "He sure did a job on himself. Who was he, Uncle Sam?"

"Don't know," Longarm said. "The Frog had something stuck in his throat, so he couldn't tell me."

Longarm knelt and felt in the soggy pockets of the green pants. The bomber had some loose change and a nasty-looking knife, but no I.D.

The copper said, "They told us about you and the case you're on. I'd say this stiff would have stood as tall as you before he got so short."

Longarm nodded. "I follow your drift. It's hard to say if he ever had a mustache like mine. But he could have been the gent who got the Teaneck Kid out of the Tombs. The one upstairs was a hired gun who owed me a disfavor. This is sure disgusting."

"Disgusting? Hell, Longarm, you just put two of the gang in the box!"

"Yeah, but not their leader—the infernal Teaneck Kid. And I might have just killed the only gents in town I could *connect* to the son of a bitch!"

Longarm didn't get much sleep that night. He had to go to Police Headquarters and explain all the noise. Mulligan and

Wojensky were off duty and at home, but the night detective squad was equally interested.

It was daybreak when he got back to his hotel. He knew that if he went to bed now he might oversleep his noon date with Monica Van Tassel. So he did the next best thing. He ran a hot tub and got in with some reading material. The hot soak would put new life in his bones and reading would keep him from falling asleep in the tub.

The wire from his Denver office was tedious. Billy Vail said the big boo from Treasury was starting to cool off and that it would be safe to head back in about a week. So a week was all the office was giving him.

A perfumed note from Madame Alice said that she wanted to see him. She said she might have a tip for him. She'd be asleep at this hour, too. He'd look her up after the luncheon party.

The New York Social Register was even duller to read than Billy Vail's wire and not much more informative than Madame Alice's message.

There was nobody named Teaneck rich enough to get their names in the fool book, but there were more Ten Ecks than you could shake a stick at. As far as he could see, none of them had ever gotten in trouble with the law or done anything else important. Ten Ecks didn't *do* things; they *owned* things. The social register tallied the Hes from the Shes, but didn't describe anyone. It seemed more important to high society who your grandfolks were than what you looked like.

He turned to the section on Vans and, sure enough, old Monica Van Tassel and her kin were in the book. Her maiden name had been De Witt and her Aunt Matilda had married a gent named Hoover, who'd just about made it. Monica's late husband had been rich and important, as Longarm had already figured out. The late Fred Hoover, Senior had been New York Dutch, which counted for something, but he'd only owned steamboats, not land, so he only rated a couple of lines. The tub water was getting tepid by this time. Longarm tossed the snob list aside and got out.

He was still uncomfortable about high society when he showed up at Monica's just before noon. He'd bought a black silk necktie and a new hickory shirt. But Monica took him upstairs to her master bedroom and showed him a boiled shirt, cutaway coat, and silly little hat she wanted him to wear. She'd already put on a lightweight beige party dress, so she told him to get cracking. Longarm looked dubious. "Don't worry," Monica said. "I know what you're thinking, but my late husband was much smaller than you. I just had these things delivered from Stewart's."

He said, "I figured they come from somewhere. I'll wear the shirt and coat, for I see my sixgun can ride as well under it. But I'll be whipped with snakes before I'll wear that fool hat!"

She started to argue, then shrugged. "Let's compromise. It's only a short way, so you can go bareheaded."

He agreed, and she left him to get gussied up. He joined her downstairs in a while, looking like a dude and feeling foolish. Monica had sandwiches prepared on the rosewood table. She said they'd best eat something before they went. It was supposed to be a luncheon, but the folks where they were going were notoriously miserly with their refreshments. He asked, in that case, why anybody went to their fool gatherings.

Monica sighed and said, "I really don't know, but we always have. The Van Pattons have been serving weak tea and tasteless potato salad since before the Revolution. George Washington once had lunch where we're going."

"Did he ever go back?"

She laughed. "No. But he didn't have to. He was only the President of the United States, not a member of Patroon Society."

Monica, or her cook, made right good sandwiches. It was hard to say how many servants she had. None of them dared to show their faces unless she rang for them. He figured they could likely make love on the Persian rug without anyone noticing. He wondered why he considered that. The high-toned widow woman wasn't acting like she wanted to. She still hadn't put any paint or powder on, even to go to a party. It was a warm day and he was already uncomfortable in the boiled shirt she'd made him wear, but she looked cool and comfortable and still smelled like a spring meadow. He wondered how she did that. Everything else in New York City smelled mighty pungent. Her perfume must be expensive as hell.

The snooty butler came in on tiptoe to announce that their carriage was out front. Longarm hadn't known they were expecting one, but she got up, so he did, too.

He escorted her outside and they got into the open carriage to ride up Fifth Avenue. It was kind of ridiculous. They only went about three blocks before they had to get out again.

As he helped her up a flight of marble steps fit for a state house he saw a couple of stern-looking gents in livery posted to keep the common folk out. But Monica just swept past them with Longarm and they never asked who he was.

Inside, they found themselves in a glass-roofed space that couldn't make up its mind if it was a garden or a railroad depot. There was a marble fountain in the middle with clipped trees growing around it in a circle of big tubs. A linen-covered buffet table ran along one wall, but nobody was paying any attention to it. The place was cluttered up with men and women who looked like they never had to shit.

They all seemed to know Monica, so Longarm had to be introduced. It wasn't as bad as he'd been braced for. They all had good manners as well as money and ancestors. They acted like Longarm was one of them. He was glad he'd worn the boiled shirt and the sissy coat. Only one man asked what Longarm did, and when he said he worked for the government the gent seemed satisfied.

Monica drew him aside under a captive palm tree and said, "You're doing fine. Did you see how that silly Mrs. Vandermeer looked at us? She's dying to ask where I found such a handsome escort."

146

"Don't tell her. You'll never live it down. When do I get to meet me some Ten Ecks?"

Monica looked around, pointed out a fat woman in a funny hat, and said that she was one. Longarm shook his head and said he'd pass on that Ten Eck.

Peter Dekker, the broker, spotted them as he came in the door. He looked startled to see Longarm there. Monica called him over and said, "You know Deputy Long, of course. Have you seen Corny Ten Eck anywhere in this crowd, Peter?"

Dekker nodded. "As a matter of fact, I think I just saw him over by the entrance. Wait here: I'll get him for you."

As the broker left, Longarm asked who Corny was. "His name's really Cornelius," Monica explained. "He's a very nice, albeit a bit odd."

"How so, odd?"

"He shoots things. Water bucks, elephants, buffalo, and so forth. He's even got a funny little creature called a dik-dik mounted in his trophy room. I'm sure I can't see why. It's a tiny antelope about the size of a fox terrier. I asked him if he'd shot it or hit it with a fly swatter, and he said women didn't understand anything about sportsmanship. I fear he's right. He's always off somewhere, hunting down wild creatures."

Longarm's eyes narrowed thoughtfully. "Has he been out of town a good spell recently, Miss Monica?"

"As a matter of fact, he just returned from a long expedition to Africa. Let me see, he must have been there at least three years. My late husband was still alive the last time we gave him a farewell dinner."

Peter Dekker came back, wearing a puzzled smile. "That's odd. I can't seem to find Corny anywhere. I may have been mistaken, but I thought I'd seen him just a few minutes ago."

Longarm asked, "What does he look like?"

Dekker frowned and said, "Rather ordinary chap. Average height and build. Why?"

147

"I want to talk to him. Do you know where he lives?"

"Certainly. He's a client of mine. I manage his business when he's out of town. He lives just up the avenue. I'll go with you if you like."

Longarm shook his head. "Just give me the address. You and Miss Monica wait here."

The broker took out a business card and pencil to scribble the house number as he asked what this was all about.

Longarm said, "I'll explain when I get back. If I get back."

Then he was moving out at a fast clip. Outside he got his bearings and headed north along Fifth Avenue. He spotted a pair of uniformed coppers shading under an elm at the edge of the park across the way. He hailed them over and told them who he was and where they were going.

It didn't take long. Like Dekker had said, the Ten Eck house was very close. One copper went around to cover the back as Longarm and the other one went up the steps and knocked.

A skinny old butler answered. Longarm asked if Cornelius Ten Eck was to home. The butler looked sort of wistful as he said, "Master Cornelius left this morning for India, sir. Tigers, I believe, this time."

"Do tell. How come he was just at the party down the avenue?"

"I'm sure I can't say, Sir. I thought he had a ship to catch this morning. But he may have had time to pay a few social calls before he left."

"You mind if we sort of look about inside?"

The butler hesitated. The copper who was with Longarm said, "We could come back with a warrant. But that'd get in the papers, wouldn't it?"

Longarm saw that the New York lawman knew more than he did about how things worked in this neck of the woods. The butler told them they could look about the house all they wanted, so they did.

Monica had been right about the dik-dik. Some of the

other creatures mounted in the oak-paneled trophy room also looked too cute for a grown man to shoot. But Ten Eck wasn't in the trophy room or any of the other rooms, not even the wine cellar. When they'd worked their way out back, the copper covering the rear entrance said nobody had passed him.

Longarm asked the old butler a few questions, found out there were no recent tintypes of the sporting Ten Eck on the premises, and told the coppers they could go to stand in the shade some more, for they'd drawn a blank.

They were about to leave when somewhere in the house a bell tinkled. Longarm stared at the butler and said, "You told us you were alone in the house, friend."

The butler said, "That's the telephone. All the fine houses along Fifth Avenue have them now."

Longarm followed him as he went to answer the bell and, sure enough, there was a new telephone set he hadn't noticed, nailed to a wall in the gloomy main hall. Longarm listened as the butler told someone else that Ten Eck was off hunting tigers and hung up. Longarm asked who it had been and the butler said he didn't know; it had been a man's voice. The trail was cold here so Longarm returned back to the party.

He found Peter Dekker still staring down the front of Monica's dress. He told her, "I have to leave on business." He expected her to say she'd let old Pete run her home, but she took his arm and said she had to go, too, so they left together.

By the time they got down the steps, her carriage had materialized as if by magic. He helped her in and, as they rode back to her place, she said, "That was close. The whole idea of your accompanying me was to establish that I didn't *need* an escort from that crowd! What's happened?"

"I may have cut a trail. I have to get me to a telephone I can use private for some calls downtown. You don't have one, do you?"

"Of course."

When they got to her home, she led him back upstairs and showed him the set in her dressing room, next to the room she slept in.

It took him more than one call before he got the right steamship line. They said they had sold passage to Liverpool to a Cornelius Ten Eck and that, if he was on this ship, he was out on the Atlantic a ways by now.

Longarm hung up and muttered curses under his breath. "It works two ways," he told Monica. "Either he caught the ship or he didn't. If he's on the high seas I'll never catch him now. If he didn't make the boat, he's still in town, but I doubt he'll come now. So I'm right back where I started!"

She asked, "Couldn't you cable the Liverpool police?"

He started to shake his head, then reconsidered. "I'd forgotten about the Atlantic Cable. You're right! It'll take him eight or ten days to cross the ocean, and we have an extradition treaty with Great Britain! You're sure smart, Miss Monica!"

"Thank you. I can have one of the maids take the cable down to the office and pay."

Longarm wrote down the message. He told the Liverpool police to be on the lookout for a possible murder suspect and that the U. S. Government would be much obliged if they'd hang on to him for a spell. When the maid had left with the message, he said to Monica, "Wonders never cease. At the rate modern science is going, in a few more years it'll be almost impossible to be an outlaw."

Monica said she certainly hoped so. New York had become a much more dangerous place than she remembered from her childhood. Then she asked if he wanted to take off the duds she'd made him wear.

He nodded, stood up, and peeled off the coat before he took her in his arms and kissed her.

She kissed him back, warmly and tenderly. But then she pushed him away and gasped, "Heavens! What are we *doing*, Custis?"

"You said to get undressed. I can see I might have took that at more than face value."

She laughed, sort of wildly, and said, "Good heavens, I never meant . . ." Then she blushed red as a rose and added, "I don't *think* I meant it that way, Custis. I'm terribly confused. I'm not used to having men just take me in their arms and kiss me."

"I noticed. I didn't figure you was fixing to grab *me*, even if you wanted to. But if you don't want to, we'll say no more about it."

She nodded, but said, "Don't be angry with me. A woman has needs, too, and I did find myself responding to you, to my considerable surprise. But, ah, can't we study on this, as you say, dear?"

He said that was fine with him. So she went out while he shucked the fancy stuff and put himself back together again. He went down to rejoin her, but he had places to go. She said she had to go to an opera that night. He said he'd study on that and, now that he knew she had a telephone, he'd call her later to say if he could make it or not. She walked him to the door and didn't struggle when he kissed her again. So he was feeling sort of springy as he walked down the steps.

But the mood faded fast. She'd called the infernal telephone operator dear, too, and he didn't think he'd enjoy opera all that much. Monica was a good old gal and that last kiss had been a humdinger. But she was the kind a man had to spend a long time getting next to, and it could take even longer getting rid of gals like that. Longarm admired women too much to want a nice gal stuck on a man with such an uncertain future. Kim Stover had never understood that, and it had left them both with burnt spots on the rug.

He was getting the hang of New York City, now. Madame Alice's place in Hell's Kitchen was a fair walk or a short cab ride through more traffic than he admired on a hot windless afternoon. He decided he'd save a quarter mile by cutting across the Central Park on foot.

It was cooler under the trees. Others had noticed it, too. But, being a weekday, there weren't many other folks in the park as he followed a footpath winding between the green trees and big elephant-hide rocks. A sassy squirrel sat up like a begging dog in front of him. Longarm laughed and said, "It's a good thing this ain't West-by-God-Virginia, squirrel. You'd have wound up in the pot by now for sure."

The Central Park was a big fake. It looked like wild countryside, but all the animals were tame. It was safe to be a duck or squirrel in here despite the woodsy stretch he was in right now. Hunting was not allowed among these trees and rocks.

Then a rifle sang out and a humming high-powered slug ticked the brim of his Stetson. Longarm dove headfirst into the nearest bushes, drawing on the fly. He crashed through the brush, rolled, and came up gun in hand, facing back the other way. He saw the faint blue haze of gunsmoke hanging above a house-sized boulder a hundred yards away. He commenced to circle in under cover from other rocks and brush. By the time he got to the top of the outcrop, the gunsmoke was gone and so was everybody else.

He heard a distant police whistle. He shrugged, holstered his gun, and gave it up for now. He wasn't about to catch a man who'd likely played all over this big park growing up. And it was getting obvious that the rascal would come looking for him again sooner or later.

# Chapter 11

Madame Alice was waiting in her red room, naked as a jaybird. He'd noticed what a hot day it was, so he took his duds off, too. As he took her in his arms, Madame Alice said, "I don't want to get all sweated up. Let's do it dog-style."

He watched, bemused, as she moved over to the bed, climbed aboard on her hands and knees, and waggled her pale rump for attention. Between her bawdy display and the awkwardness at Monica's house, he was at attention all over as he stepped up behind her, took a hip in each hand, and just sort of eased inside. It was even hotter in there, but not at all uncomfortable.

Madame Alice said, "Oh, that feels good," and it was a nice cool way to do it.

As they cuddled naked together afterwards, Longarm

said to Madame Alice, "You said you had something else you wanted to see me about?"

"I heard about that fellow who blew himself up behind your hotel. I think he might have been a no-good called Dandy Williams."

"Tell me about him."

"He started as a pimp. The girl who told me about it remembered those yellow shoes. He was a mean bastard, even for a pimp. A while back he was sent up the river for beating one of his girls so bad she pressed charges. They say that in the Big House he teamed up with another man and learned to handle explosives."

"The gent who tried to bomb me a second time knew more than most but less than he should have about handling dynamite. I like his name, too."

"Hell, honey, he probably made that up. Nobody on the street ever uses their right name."

"I noticed. The Teaneck Kid sassed us with Tweed. Mr. Frog said to call him Marcy. Now this pimp turned bomber turns out to be Williams. It fits. William Marcy Tweed, the biggest crook the three of them ever heard of. It sounds like some sort of kids' gang deal."

"Where does Teaneck fit in?"

Longarm lit up one of his cheroots as he explained. "Teaneck is a sort of inside insult to the high-and-mighty Ten Eck family. The Teaneck Kid seems to have a warped sense of humor. If he's who it's starting to look like, he skates on mighty thin ice for a gent who shoots rabbit-sized antelope. I reckon he got bored with being proper so he took to seeking adventures. Only the guns was loaded with real ammo and the game got rough."

He brought her up to date. She sighed and said, "Well, if you have the rat who told them you were coming, and the taller one who pretended to be you, and if the English coppers will be waiting on the Liverpool docks for the last member of the gang, that means you won't be in town much longer, huh?"

It meant no such thing. But he didn't point out that one

person still at large had just taken a shot at him. He didn't want to hurt her feelings, but he saw little reason to come back here, even if she was so friendly. She took his silence as agreement and sighed. "I want to remember you right. Can we do it old-fashioned again, sweat and all, before you leave?"

"In a minute. I didn't get any sleep last night, and I'd best finish this cheroot and get my breath back."

She said to go ahead and puff while she enjoyed a fatter cigar. So he lay back, blowing smoke rings, as she proceeded to blow him. She did that mighty nice, too. So, not wanting to waste it on her tonsils, he snuffed out his smoke, rolled her over, and boarded her right.

She'd been right. They got sweaty as hell. But she let him use her bathtub before he left, and, seeing as he was leaving, she got in with him so's they could clean up while they stayed dirty together.

As he left Hell's Kitchen, Longarm was beginning to see why New Yorkers were in such a hurry all the time. There was something wrong with the clocks here. It was always later than you thought. But he was getting the hang of it. He stopped in a cigar store, strode over to Broadway, and caught a street car downtown. It gave him more time to think.

When he got off at Broadway and Wall Street, Detectives Mulligan and Wojensky were waiting for him. He took a card from his pocket, read the address, and said, "Let's go. I'll fill you in on the way."

They fell in with him, and Mulligan asked where they were going. Longarm said, "To arrest the gent who impersonated me at the Tombs."

"I thought that was the tall guy who was blown apart behind your hotel."

"It wasn't. He wouldn't have dared. I just found out he was likely a former pimp turned safecracker called Dandy Williams. Ever heard of him?"

"I know him," Wojensky said. "He's a real bastard. He

preyed on women, but he didn't *like* them much, if you know what I mean."

"I'm ahead of you. That bounty hunter, Marcy, had a chance at a handsome female I know for a fact was willing. She'd have likely said no to a man as ugly as *him,* but he never tried. He had her at his mercy, naked and in irons, too."

Mulligan said, "Some guys are like that. But it's strange that you tripped over a pal of the gang, of all people, on your way to New York."

"No, it wasn't. He was on another case, operating out of Chicago. But gents like that have a sort of network or grapevine. They have to. For some reason they take crimes against nature more seriously than some crimes against people and property, so a sissy can be put away for twenty years in most states. Marcy must have lived in New York once. Likely as a kid, if he admired Tweed so. As a wandering bounty hunter hunter he likely sometimes returned to New York and looked up old buddies. When he found out I was after one, he warned 'em by wire."

"Aw, come on! The Teaneck Kid shot a man over a woman!"

"He's likely double gaited, like the man we're after, and the late Dandy Williams. Marcy was what you might call an honest sissy, which is why he blustered so when he wasn't playing gal. The Kid just screwed anybody, any way he could. He got along fine with the old cons at Leavenworth and mayhaps got a guard's gun by acting sissy. Some guards get lonely, too. Teaneck might have only been after that rich married woman's money. Anyway, like I said, old boys like that keep in touch. When Marcy wired I was on my way but sort of taking my time, they wired him to come East and join them again in case they needed an extra gun. Marcy was a sissy, but he was a hired gun, too."

They came to the building Longarm was looking for and he led them in. As they rode up in the hydraulic elevator, Mulligan asked Longarm who they were going to visit.

"A broker named Peter Dekker," Longarm said. "They

say he handles all of Cornelius Ten Eck's business. It's sure starting to look that way. He gave me his business card, too. We're just about going to make it before closing time."

Mulligan said, "Wait a minute. I know Peter Dekker. I don't know if he's queer or not, but he looks nothing like you, Longarm!"

"Sure he does. He's my height and build. Anyone can put on a Stetson and a false mustache, right?"

"Jesus, he was sure taking a chance for a client!"

"He had to, most likely. Aside from their mutual interests, the Kid knew Dekker was churning the stocks and bonds of other important folk. I caught him giving poor advice to a poor old widow woman. Took me a spell to sort it out. He sent me on a wild goose chase and then took a shot at me in the park."

"How do you know it was him?"

"Had to be. The only other suspect to the ambush was a gal, and she'd just had me at her mercy. He lurked in the park across from her front door and followed me to gun me down. Lucky for me he missed. I gave him plenty of time to get back down to Wall Street, of course."

They got out on the sixth floor. Longarm saw they'd timed it close, for it was just after five. As they walked toward the oak doors of the brokerage firm, the doors opened and Peter Dekker came out, followed closely by the Teaneck Kid.

The two detectives didn't know the Kid on sight, as Longarm did. So they were confused as Longarm snapped, "Both of you grab sky!"

Dekker went for the gun under his frock coat as the Teaneck Kid screamed and started running off down the corridor.

Longarm fired a couple of rounds into Dekker as the broker had his gun half out. Dekker cursed, staggered against the wall, and slid down it, slicking it with blood as, down at the far end, the glass window crashed when the bolting Teaneck Kid ran into it and kept going. It was six stories to Wall Street and he screamed all the way down.

Wojensky said, "Jesus, that was Freddy Hoover! He's from a fine old Patroon family uptown!"

Longarm sighed and said, "Do tell? That wraps her up pretty good, then. I have to get to a telegraph office, pronto. An innocent man named Cornelius Ten Eck is fixing to get a dismal surprise when he arrives in Liverpool if I don't explain to the English law how these two tried to set him up."

Wojensky followed Longarm to the window. "Are you saying one of the fancy Ten Ecks is mixed up with this crazy gang?" he asked.

Longarm looked out and down. The Teaneck Kid lay like a stepped-on bug in a circle of excited pedestrians. He saw a couple of uniformed coppers pushing through to take charge of the mess on the sidewalk.

He pulled his head in and said, "No, but they tried to make me think so. I went to a fancy party uptown earlier today. Dekker, back there, came in and must have shit his britches when he saw me there. He knew his pal, Fred Hoover, would come in any second, and that I'd recognize him as the Teaneck Kid from out West.

"But he was one cool cuss. He tried to play a shell game on me by implying Corny Ten Eck was the one who'd lit out on learning I was there. He knew Ten Eck had left town to go off hunting again. So he aimed me at Ten Eck's house, where he knew I'd be unable to compare notes and would likely get even more suspicious.

"I started to. But, as I mulled it over in my head, a mess of things wouldn't work. Ten Eck was sort of a mystery man about his comings and goings, but he was too damned rich to steal Indian beef even for fun. And what fun could chasing cows be for a man who'd already shot an elephant?"

"Sooner or later you'd have been able to check on whether or not Ten Eck had been to Africa, like he said, or somewhere out West," Wojensky remarked.

"Sure, but they had to gain time and they didn't aim to let me live long enough. Ten Eck's already been out West. A spell back, from the looks of the prime buffalo head and prairie bighorn he had mounted in his trophy room. There ain't been bighorn on the high plains for over five years and the buffalo herds are thinned mighty ragged. His buffalo was a big herd bull old enough to have a fearsome spread of horn. So, after someone missed me with an easy rifle shot in the park, I knew it couldn't be no dedicated hunter who's been picking off everything from elephants to little bitty antelope at long range all his adult life."

Longarm lit a smoke and stared soberly at the body of Dekker on the floor. "The Teaneck Kid was better with a gun than this poor bastard, too. So it had to be Dekker. He used the telephone in the Van Patton house to call the Kid and tell him to meet him here. Then he tried to gun me, messed up, and come down to join the Kid for a strategy meeting. You boys know the rest."

Mulligan took a whistle from his pocket, blew it out the window, waved, and came back to say, "No, we don't, Longarm. I see how this poor sissy could recruit like-minded riff-raff like Marcy and Williams. But how in hell did he wind up with a society swell like Freddy Hoover?"

"That's the easy part," Longarm said. "Freddy Hoover *wasn't* all that swell. He was a poor relation. He never got to go on elephant hunts and such with the rich kids he growed up with. He must have been jealous of Ten Eck and his way of going off to all sorts of exciting places to return with trophy heads and tales of glory. He wanted to be a Ten Eck, too. He couldn't be a real Ten Eck, but he *could* be the Teaneck Kid. So he went out West to play desperado and he desperadoed himself right into Leavenworth.

"When he was arrested he made up another name so his friends and neighbors back here wouldn't know of his disgrace. He escaped and came back. He come to his old pal Pete Dekker, yonder. Dekker staked him and helped him fit back into society. But the kid was naturally nasty, and wound up shooting another man.

"So when another old buddy of theirs wired I was on my way here to pick his pal up, and told Dekker what I looked like, Dekker saw his chance. He bought a hat and false mustache and typed up some legal-looking papers on the fancy machinery any broker has on hand. He bluffed the kid out of jail and sent him home to his dotty momma up in patroon country—the last place anyone would expect to find an escaped murderer."

"Why didn't they quit while they were ahead? You'd never have found him if they'd left you alone."

Longarm nodded. "I've wondered about that on other cases as well. I reckon if folks had the brains to avoid messing with the law, they wouldn't get to be outlaws in the first place. Marcy had his own reasons for not liking me. Meanwhile they asked Dandy Williams for help while old Fred lay low. They hoped to get me before I stumbled over anything. They were planning to get the Teaneck Kid out of town some expensive way we'll have to guess at, knowing only that he was putting the bite on rich kin. Hell, Mulligan, there's always a few loose ends when you wipe all the bad guys out. What more do you need?"

The elevator door opened and a squad of coppers came out. Mulligan said, "Nothing. It's time to drag the whole mess to the watch commander and wrap it up tidy."

It got a bit more complicated than that. They let Longarm cable Liverpool from Police Headquarters. He wired Billy Vail a sort of brag while he was about it. Then he found a telephone took a deep breath, and asked the operator to hook him up with Monica Van Tassel.

She answered on the second ring. Her voice sounded more weary than sad as she said, "I'm afraid our opera date is off, dear. I just had terrible news about my Cousin Freddy. Going out in public tonight would be out of the question."

"I was just going to tell you about it," he said. "I'm at Police Headquarters. How's your aunt taking it?"

"Hysterically, of course. I just came from there. Fortunately, a whole flock of dear old biddies came there to comfort her about Fred's accident. So I was able to slip away. I've never really liked Fred, but it seems a poor time to be celebrating, so . . ."

160

"Hold on," he cut in, frowning. "Did you say you thought your cousin was killed *accidental*, Miss Monica?"

"Well, wasn't he? I haven't heard all the details, but it's my understanding that he fell out of a window while the police were having a gunfight with Peter Dekker. Do you know what really happened, dear?"

He said, "Yeah. What say I come up in a while to sort of explain it to you in detail?"

"I'd like that, Custis. I'll be expecting you."

He hung up and walked into the ward room where the detectives and their captain were exchanging congratulations.

"Time for a fresh deck, gents," he said. "I don't like the way we put it down on paper the first time, so we're going to have to word a few things different."

The captain frowned. "I've got a hundred reporters out front waiting for an official statement. I have to tell them something. What's wrong with the truth?"

"Sometimes the truth can hurt. I exposed the impersonator who made fools out of the police. It was me who put him down. So he's mine. On the other hand, he could be yours, if you want to deal."

The captain handed Longarm his note pad and a pencil and said, "Write it up. If it makes my boys look good, I'll sign it."

# Chapter 12

The reason New Yorkers walked so good was because their traffic moved so bad. By the time Longarm made it back uptown to Monica's house it was after dark. The air was still and even hotter as he climbed out of his cab in front of her place. The park across the way smelled stale and musty, like the trees and brush were painted scenery in an old abandoned theater with a leaking roof. It had to be fixing to storm. New York was never going to make it through this hot summer night unless God opened the windows and let some air in.

He went up the stairs walking chipper enough but feeling like he'd been hauled through the keyhole backwards. The lack of sleep and the letdown were starting to hit him, now. The hunt was over. Skinning out and salting the game was just a tedious chore. But cleaning up after a hunt was part of the deal.

Monica Van Tassel must have been watching for him. She opened the door herself. Longarm wondered what had happened to her butler.

She was wearing a modest bathrobe. As she led him inside she said, "I hope you'll overlook my state of dress. I've taken two baths since I came home from Aunt Matilda's and I'm already sticky again."

"It'll likely start raining fire and salt in a minute," he said.

"I know. I grew up in this climate. The only thing to be said for New York weather is that if you don't like it, you only have to wait a few minutes."

By this time they were going up the stairs to the floor above. He didn't ask why. He figured she'd tell him why. She did. She said, "I'm not receiving visitors this evening, so I don't want the lamps lit in the downstairs front windows."

She led him into her master bedroom. The four-poster across the room was discreetly curtained. A tea set sat on a teakwood chest in front of a silk brocaded sofa. They sat down and she started pouring tea as she said, "Tell me what happened. I can't believe Peter Dekker was shot by the police. When I got the news I had a rather desperate look at my stock portfolio, but it seems to be in order. Peter hasn't lost any money for me since he's been handling my late husband's estate."

"He wasn't out and out robbing his clients," Longarm said. "He was too slick for that. But he was churning accounts more than he should have."

"Churning? Is that something illegal?"

"No, but it ought to be. The exchange is going to be mighty vexed with old Pete as they examine his books. But it's a mite late to take his brokerage license away. A churner is a broker who uses his discretionary power over a client's money to buy and sell stocks and bonds more than he really has to. Have a real accountant go over your portfolio and you'll find out that, while he didn't lose money for you, he cost you a heap of interest and dividends by swapping

164

back and forth instead of letting your blue chips lay and just grow natural. His profit in churning you and his other clients was the brokerage fee he pocketed every time he traded, say, a steamship share for a railroad bond."

She nodded. "Oh, I see how it works. I never liked Peter, anyway. I might have known he was a sneak. But where does poor Cousin Freddy fit in, and just how did he die? I've spoken to our family lawyer on the telephone and he says he's confused, too."

Longarm took a sip of tea. He had to stay awake, and the tea might help. "It's kind of complicated, but the official story, as it will be printed in the newspapers, was that Pete Dekker was more than a sneak. He was a confederate of the Teaneck Kid. So we went to his office to arrest him. Meanwhile, your cousin, Fred Hoover, was on his way to have it out with Dekker about some other crooked business. Fred must have figured out Dekker was churning his friends and relations. So he went downtown to tell him he'd best cut it out. That's what Fred was doing there when the police showed up to arrest the rascal. We told the reporters Fred Hoover was an innocent bystander who got shoved out the window in the confusion."

She frowned thoughtfully at him and asked, soberly, "Is that the whole truth, Custis? You're forgetting I grew up with Cousin Freddy."

Longarm shrugged. "Cousin Fred couldn't tell us, personal, that he'd gone down there to defend his friends and family against a Wall Street scoundrel. But he could have, and it makes him look good in the *Sun*, so why worry about the fine print? The case is over and everyone else is satisfied. You ought to be, too."

She sighed and said, "Well, I never expected Freddy Hoover to die as even a modest hero. But wait, your case *can't* be over. You still haven't caught your Teaneck Kid. He's on the high seas on his way to Liverpool, isn't he?"

"Nope. Pete Dekker tried to frame old Corny Ten Eck. I cabled Liverpool that it was a mistake. So Ten Eck is free to go play with his tigers. The real Teaneck Kid must have hated old Corny. Corny Ten Eck's sort of odd to folks like you and me, but some admire men like him, and he was the real thing. He didn't play over there in the park or hang about Cow Town a few blocks away to feel adventurous. He had money in his pants and hair on his chest to adventure real, starting in his teen years. The reporters were telling me about him. The rascal was allowed to use his family's hunting lodge in the Maine woods when he was just a tad. Shot his first moose at ten and made a rug out of a grownup bear at eleven. Think how the other kids must have *envied* him, Miss Monica.

"Corny Ten Eck was the kind of boy every boy dreams of being. He was shooting game, sailing his own boat, riding his own thoroughbreds before most of his rich little friends was allowed to play in the park across the way without their nannies. He got to go out West and shoot buffalo when he was still in prep school and Red Cloud's Dakota was still taking scalps. Lord, how that must have smarted when the stay-at-homes heard about it!"

Monica sniffed. "I remember. Personally, I thought it was rather juvenile then, and I still do. None of us are children any more. Corny is only a few years older than me, so he must be at least thirty by now."

"Do tell? Thought you was mayhaps twenty-one or -two, Miss Monica."

"Forget how old I may be. If this Teaneck Kid of yours wasn't Corny Ten Eck, who was he?"

"Oh, we decided he must have been the rascal who blew his fool self up behind my hotel. I remembered hearing he favored yellow shoes. So, like I said, it's over. Both the Teaneck Kid and the impostor who helped him escape from the Tombs are dead. So's the fat rascal who murdered Miss Billie McArtle with that bomb."

He stared wisfully into space as he added, half to himself, "She sure would have had a grand story, had she lived to write it. We put her in the official report so's folks could see how she died covering the news. The *Sun's* fixing to run a nice tribute to her."

He yawned, smiled sheepishly, and said, "Sorry. I'm having a hard time keeping my eyes open. Now that you know it all, I'd best study on getting home to bed before I fall asleep on you."

There was a low rumble of distant thunder. Monica said, "You'll never make it all the way down to Canal Street before that storm hits. Why don't you sleep here?"

That woke him up, some. He stared at her.

She dimpled and added, "I meant in the guest room, of course. We've plenty of room and there's no sense in your getting soaked."

Before he could answer, there was a mighty crack of thunder and somebody seemed to be playing a fire hose against the window glass. She laughed. "See what I mean?"

He nodded and said, "I'll take you up on your kind offer. But, ah, won't the neighbors talk?"

"Pooh, what can they say—that I had a guest overnight? It's my house and my business. Besides, nobody gossips about me. I wouldn't like it."

"I can see the social disadvantages of crossing a Van Tassel. But what about your servants?"

"What about them? They work for me. Besides, they spend the night in their own wing, and even if they didn't, I see nothing improper in saving a gentleman from drowning, do you?"

"Well, not if you don't, ma'am. But can I either lay down or light out, soon? I'm getting past tired into about-to-pass-out."

She rose. "Come with me, then."

She led him to another bedroom across the hall and lit the lamp. As he stared in admiration at the furnishings, and pure longing at the big feather bed, Monica cracked the window open and said, "It will be much cooler in a little while. As I said, the coming dawn promises to be gray and wet, but comfortably cool." She saw that he didn't feel like talking about the weather and added, "I'll leave you, now. The bath is just next door. Sleep as late as you like. I'm an early riser, so just come down and join me any time in the morning, or, if you'd like your breakfast in bed, pull that cord and tell the maid when she comes."

She hesitated, nodded to herself, and went out, closing the door behind her. Longarm staggered toward the bed, shucking his duds and letting them fall anywhere they had a mind to. He hung his gun rig over a bedpost, pulled down the counterpane, and doused the lamp. The cool draft felt so good on his naked hide that it knocked him out as he sprawled across the crisp linen sheets.

Longarm didn't remember falling asleep, so he didn't know he was. He seemed to be in a big, spooky church. The organ was ringing like a telephone set, which was sort of odd when you studied on it. But it was even odder to find himself moving up the aisle arm-in-arm with a shorter figure in a bridal gown. He disremembered asking any gal to marry up with him. He couldn't see her face under the heavy white veil she wore. He wondered how in thunder he was going to get out of this fix. It seemed a mite late to call the wedding off. But, damn it, he wasn't ready to get hitched to anybody, and he didn't even know who this infernal she-male *was!*

He woke up, cussing and thrashing. He stared wildly about in the darkness, trying to remember where he was at first. Then as he listened to the rain outside and got his bearings, his heart slowed down and he started breathing sensible. It was all right. It had only been a nightmare.

He propped himself up on one elbow, wondering what time it was. It was still dark, but he was wide awake now. Longarm didn't need much sleep in the first place and didn't want another dream like that in the second. He felt he should be up and prowling about. But there wasn't anyplace that needed prowling, now. The hunt was over. He was free to spend the next few days any way he liked. Billy Vail didn't want him to come back for at least another week.

He lay back and studied on how he was to kill more time in New York without any real chores to do. He'd seen everything in the infernal place. Maybe he could sort of head back to Denver slow, stopping off to explore other wonders of the wild, wild East. If the damned rain let up, he could let himself out before anyone else here was up and about. It'd save saying goodbye and having to answer more questions that could trip him up if he neglected to mention the late Freddy Hoover respectfully.

The door opened and Monica's voice said, "Are you awake? I heard you cry out."

"I had a bad dream. I'm sorry if I woke you up, ma'am."

She came over and sat on the edge of the bed. "I've been awake for some time. My lawyer called a while ago. He got the true story out of a police official he clubs with. Naturally, neither the newspapers nor Aunt Matilda will ever know. But why did you *do* it, Custis?"

He sat up again and reached for the lamp. "You just answered your own question, ma'am. Why disgrace a fine old family and break a poor old woman's heart?"

She placed a hand on his naked forearm to warn, "Don't light the lamp. I'm not properly dressed. I've been pacing the floor in my room, dying to talk to you, but not wanting to disturb you."

Lightning flashed over the Central Park across the way and Longarm was a mite disturbed as he caught a quick glimpse of her. She had on a mighty thin nightgown, likely because the night had started out so warm. It was cool enough, now, but he didn't feel cool at all. He said, "Well, you can talk to me, now. What you you aim to talk to me about, Miss Monica?"

"I wanted to thank you. I know you allowed yourself to look bad to your superiors on our account. The lawyer told me the police are crowing about your arrest."

Longarm shrugged. "Let 'em crow. I never arrested Pete Dekker. I shot the rascal. I'm glad I didn't have to shoot your cousin, even if he was a rascal, too. I wouldn't feel right, accepting hospitality from kin of a gent I had to gun."

"It will make it easier for me to face poor Aunt Matilda in time to come. She's already making a saint of the awful brat," Monica said.

"Well, I suspicion lots of saints might not be saints if

all was known about them. I see no harm in letting the innocent remember the guilty dead fonder than they might deserve. I'm sure sorry you had to find out what really happened, Miss Monica."

"I'm not. I'm glad. I'm a mature woman and I don't have to be sheltered from the facts of life."

Then the weather made a liar out of her. A gully-whumping bolt of lightning split an elm across the avenue out front, tingling their hair and damned near splitting their eardrums. The next thing they knew, Monica was in his arms with her face buried against his bare chest, gasping like a scared little girl.

He patted her back through the thin silk and said, "There, there, it's not going to getcha inside all these rock walls."

He expected her to sit up, flustered. But she stayed snuggled against his naked chest. "I must be more upset than I thought," she whispered. "I'm not usually afraid of thunderstorms. We have them all summer, here."

"Well, the one we're having now's a caution."

There was another tremendous bolt and she flinched in his arms as he chuckled and said, "See what I mean?"

Then they were both laughing and the rain was coming down harder and it just seemed natural to pull her under the covers with him to comfort her. She snuggled close with a sigh. He lowered her head to the pillow and kissed her. She kissed him back hungrily, and his free hand went exploring down her thin silk-covered curves. But as he cupped her firm breast, massaging the turgid nipple with his palm, she stiffened and gasped, with her lips against his, "What are you doing?"

"That's a mighty dumb question, coming from an experienced widow woman. But if you want me to stop, I will."

She sighed. "I *should* tell you to stop."

"I know. But do you want me to or not? We'd better decide pronto, lest it get too late to stop, if you follow my drift."

She sighed again and said, "I'm afraid we're already in

170

trouble. You must think I'm dreadfully bold, but . . ."

He saw she was one of those gals who talked dumb about her natural feelings. So he kissed her some more to shut her up and, having pretty well decided what her breasts felt like, ran his hand down her trembling flesh while inching her thin gown up at the same time with his fingers. She didn't resist. In fact, she tongued him back at first. But then he had her gown all the way up, and, as he got to feeling up the real thing, she moaned, "Oh, stop! I have to have time to think!"

He knew if you let gals get to thinking at times like these they generally said no, then never forgave you for stopping. So he just rolled atop her, and whatever she was thinking, she opened her thighs in welcome, so he went on in.

She gasped, and then, since she must have known anything she might say would sound foolish, she just went crazy in his arms for a spell. She made love like the happily married woman she'd once been, but he could feel by her passion that she hadn't done so recently. She climaxed ahead of him, twice, and then he came and paused to get his second wind. "That was lovely," she said. "But stop a moment, darling. This is getting serious. We have to decide how we're going to go about this affair, Custis."

"Hell, girl, we're doing just fine, if you ask me. Why don't we get rid of that nightgown and do it even better?"

He rolled off and she sat up to peel the gown off over her head, with a lucky bolt of lightning showing him just how grand she looked as stark as him. But as she snuggled down against him, she said, "There are some limits to Fifth Avenue tolerance. I can't keep you here more than a night or so."

He kissed her, feeling a wave of relief, before he said, "That's all right. I won't make a pest of myself. I never stay where I ain't wanted. I can leave before daybreak, if you like."

"Good Lord, that *would* cause a scandal! Besides, I don't want you to leave. Not yet. Can I speak frankly to you, Custis?"

171

"Sure. We're pals, ain't we?"

She giggled and started exploring him some with her own hand as she said, "I suppose we must be. But, seriously, the reason I haven't taken a lover since my husband died had nothing to do with my feelings. You know they're warmer than Queen Victoria or the Patroon Society approves of. I don't want to fall in love with you, Custis. I hcpe I haven't hurt your feelings."

"Just keep moving that hand down a mite and you'll discover how mortally injured I am. I savvy the ground rules you want to set up, Monica. You want us to be pards, but nothing permanent, right?"

She grasped his erection and sighed, "Oh, you *are* still feeling friendly! I am, too. It's even nicer to know you're not going to be silly later. You've no idea how many fortune hunters I've had to fend off, darling."

"I don't hunt fortunes. I hunt owlhoots. But now that we've set up the rules, do we have to talk so cold-natured about it?"

"Bear with me a moment. How long will you be able to stay in the East?"

"I could stay a week or ten days without getting fired. But you said I couldn't stay here without ruining your reputation. You want to go back to my hotel with me?"

"Heavens, no! We'll spend a week out on the Island in a rented beach cottage. Nobody out there knows me. Would you like that, dear? I'd do the cooking and it would be just the two of us on a secluded stretch of beach..."

The Atlantic Ocean was just as big as he'd expected. Her notion of a cottage was a surprise, for it was mighty fancy. Someone had taken the dust covers off the fancy furniture and stocked the larder for a week's stay. Magical things seemed to happen when you were rich.

Monica took her duds right off and they leaped on the bed together by daylight. Then, after they'd made love a spell, she took him by the hand and led him out naked to frolic in the sea. He felt awkward at first, for they were

172

out under the open sky and you could see a mile up the beach either way. But nobody seemed to notice. They even made love in the ocean.

Monica said she enjoyed roughing it. That's what she called camping in a house a lot of folks out West would be proud to own as their home spread. Longarm thought they were shacked up mighty high on the hog, so they both enjoyed the week and a day they spent out there. She fed him fancy tinned foods he'd never seen before and, in return, he taught her a couple of positions even a once married woman found new to her.

They made love on the bed, on the kitchen table, in the bath, and everyplace else they could get to. At night they made love out under the stars on a blanket. Free from the confines of her proper friends and relations, Monica could get downright bawdy.

But time slipped by and the bittersweet ride back to the city hurt more than either of them had figured. She was quiet on the train. She held his hand and didn't say much until they were almost there. Then she said, "We'll be getting off in a minute. I think it's best if I take a cab home alone."

He nodded and said he understood.

She sighed. "No, you don't."

He didn't answer. The train was slowing, so they got up. He walked her down to the end of the car and helped her down to the platform. It was late afternoon.

"I hate goodbyes," Monica said. "Would you do me a favor? Would you just turn and walk away? Would you not look back, even if I said something silly?"

He said, "Sure. But can't you say it to my face?"

She sighed. "No. We can never meet again, darling. I've thought and thought about it, but it just wouldn't work."

He nodded and said, "I know. I know how to think, too. It's been nice knowing you, Monica. Have a nice life, hear?"

She nodded silently, so he turned away and started walking. Behind him, her voice was low as she murmured, "I love you, Custis."

173

But she'd asked him not to look back, so he didn't. He just kept walking, swallowing the lump in his throat as the treacherous summer breeze followed him with a faint hint of perfume that smelled like fresh spring meadowland, and the memory of a sun-kissed nude sea goddess, frolicking in the waves, far away and already all too long ago.

# Chapter 13

Denver smelled more like burning leaves than ever when Longarm met Marshal Billy Vail at the Union Depot. Vail said, "Well, Treasury is after someone else, now. The trouble with having a tedious disposition is that you're always getting sore at somebody new. Let's go up to the Black Cat and inhale some beer whilst you tell me how you messed up this time."

"I hardly ever mess up, Billy," Longarm said. "I got to stay here till they unload the baggage car. They said they had to take the coffin I shipped off last, to avoid unsettling the other passengers."

One of the other passengers getting off was a handsome brunette gal with a polka-dot parasol and matching Dolly Vardin skirt. She smiled as she passed and Longarm ticked the brim of his Stetson to her before telling Vail, "It'll only take a minute, now. Don't worry, the coffin's lead lined and I told 'em to go heavy on the rock salt."

Vail frowned. "I know how to ship cadavers, damn it. But who in hell did you bring back? The papers say the New York police released the body of that impostor you shot to be buried by his kin."

"I know. They had to. He was an important Wall Street gent. We had to let them bury the—ah—innocent bystander in New York, too. But you told me not to come back without the Teaneck Kid and the man who impersonated a Federal officer, didn't you?"

"You're damned right! And I've been meaning to talk to you about that. You let the New York law have both the rascals. All you was allowed to keep was that fat-ass bounty hunter and the pimp who blowed himself to hash. Which one have you got aboard this infernal train, the fat one or what's left of the skinny one?"

Longarm fished out a smoke, lit it up, and said, "Let's mosey up and see if we can have the box, now. We'll have it drayed over to the morgue so's we can get a photograph for the files before we plant the son of a bitch in Potter's Field. I sent the Teaneck Kid's cadaver to Leavenworth, so's they can close that part of the case official. The gent I brung home with me was the impostor, a broker named Pete Dekker."

Vail said, "Damn it, I know who Dekker was. It was in the papers. But how in hell can he be *here*, if his kin buried him in New York like the papers said? Goddamnit, Longarm, have you tried to slicker the U. S. Government with a body switch?"

"Of course not. That would be a Federal crime and you warned me never to do that no more. I give you my word I come back with the real impostor and the real Teaneck Kid's on his way to Leavenworth."

"Damn it, you must have slickered *someone*, then!"

Longarm grinned sheepishly and said, "I had to. You see, there was four bodies in the morgue. The Hoovers and Dekkers were clamoring to bury two of them. Nobody gave a shit about the dead pimp and bounty hunter. So me and a nice New York copper named Wojensky had a long talk with a pal of his in the morgue and, well, young Hoover was easy. We already had us a cadaver that was so messed up his momma wouldn't want to look at him. The pimp. So we gave him to the Teaneck Kid's momma and she opted for a closed-casket ceremony, too. She'd heard her innocent child landed on cement after a mighty long fall. Before you cloud up and rain all over me, I never busted any *Federal* regulation in letting the Hoovers bury that mangled pimp. Somebody had to bury the rascal and I only swindled pure civilians."

Vail laughed. "You're incredible! What about this other one you brung home to lay on my back doorstep, you grinning tomcat?"

"That took more skill. The official report just said he'd been shot resisting arrest. So they let me shoot him a couple more times as he lay on the morgue slab. After that, he needed a closed casket, too. Old Marcy was a lot shorter, but he weighed as much or more as Dekker, so the pallbearers never noticed."

By now they'd reached the last of the cars and, sure enough, the baggage smashers were loading a lead-foil-sheathed coffin on a dray. Longarm said, "All's well that ends well. The kin got to bury somebody. The useless skunks got buried better than they deserved. The Justice Department has the sons of bitches I was sent to get. Ain't you going to tell me how smart I am?"

Vail frowned. "Hold on. The New York police have handed out a different version to the newspapers."

"Sure they have. *They* like to look good, too. Our files are meant to be kept accurate and official, not to get our names in the papers. We only report to Washington, not the New York *Sun*. In the time to come, someone may notice a few discrepancies, but who cares? The case is closed for all the lawmen concerned, one damned way or another."

He turned from Vail to tell the drayman where he wanted the coffin brought. This gave Billy Vail time to think. So

177

as the dray pulled out, he nodded. "By God, it works! Come on, old son, I'm taking you up to the Black Cat to buy you that drink, now. You done good and I'm mighty pleased with you, you loco bastard!"

Longarm said, "I'd admire having a drink with you some other time, but if you really want to do me a favor, could I have the rest of the day off?"

Vail frowned, looked up at the sun, and said, "I reckon you've earned it. But is it too much to ask what you had in mind? You just got here, and it's early as hell to study on going home to bed."

"I ain't tired. I got more sleep than I needed aboard the train. My luck was awful, coming back. But, well, did you notice that gal getting off with the parasol, back there?"

"I did, and she's a looker. Have you been messing with her, Longarm?"

"Not yet. I just met her this morning in the dining car. I don't know how the hell I missed her earlier. She says she's just come out from back East. She's a tourist gal on her vacation. She mentioned that she's dying to see the wild, wild West and that she'll be staying in Denver a spell. I sent her to that hotel near the Federal Building."

"The one that don't ask questions?"

"Of course. I owed it to the room clerk. He's a pal of mine. Anyway, what I had in mind for the rest of the day..."

"Say no more," Vail cut in, adding, "I know all too well what you have in mind. Poor little gal will likely never see Pike's Peak, now. But I suspicion you'll show her some other big rises of the West, right?"

Longarm sighed. "I sure hope so. I got some forgetting to do about that trip back East, Billy."

"Do tell? I figured you'd find it a restful change. You likely found it so restful it got tedious, huh? I might have known you'd find it dull to mix with all them New York City sissies."

Longarm started to say he hadn't found the East as sissy as he'd expected. But he didn't want to disillusion his boss,

178

and if he didn't catch up with that flirty gal pronto, someone else was likely to wind up showing her the wild West. So he lit out, walking New York City style. He laughed as he caught sight of himself reflected in a glass window, but he didn't slow down. There was something to be said for both kinds of wildness.

Watch for

**LONGARM IN THE BIG BEND**

fiftieth novel in the bold
LONGARM series from Jove

*coming in December!*

F

## MORE ROUGH RIDING ACTION FROM JOHN WESLEY HOWARD